CW00330028

# THE WICKED WILL

# PERISH 3

# *THE ASSASSIN*

## By

## Anthony Vincent Bruno

## © 2014

THE WICKED WILL PERISH 3 - THE ASSASSIN

A thriller by Anthony Vincent Bruno

©2014 by Anthony Vincent Bruno

Paperback ISBN: 9781790411818

All rights reserved. No part of this book may be reproduced without written permission, except for brief quotations to books and critical reviews. This story is a work of fiction. Characters and events are a product of the author's imagination. Any resemblance to persons, living or dead is purely coincidental.

A CIP catalogue record for this title is available from the British Library.

# CONTENTS

## GLOSSARY

AK-47 – Kalashnikov gas-operated, $7.62 \times 39$mm assault rifle

APC - Armoured Personnel Carrier

AQT - al Qaeda Taleban

Bootneck - Royal Marine Commando

Browning 9mm – Hi power single action semi-automatic handgun

Casevac - Casualty Evacuation

COBRA – Cabinet Office briefing room A. UK crisis committee

CFT - Combat Fitness Test

Claymore - Portable anti-personnel mine

CO - Commanding Officer

C019 - Metropolitan Police Specialist Firearm Unit

Det cord - Detonating cord

FOB - Forward Operating Base

Flash bang - Stun grenade

GCHQ - Government Communications HQ

Gimpy or GPMG - General Purpose Machine Gun

GPS - Global Positioning System

HK MP5 - Heckler and Koch counter-terrorist sub machine gun

Icom - Intelligence communication

IED - Improvised explosive device

IR - Infrared

Klick - Kilometre

L109A1 - Fragmentation Grenade with a fuse delay of 3.4 seconds

L96A1 - Long range sniper rifle

LZ - Landing zone

MI5 – Secret Service, UK domestic counter-intelligence service

MI6 – Secret Intelligence Service, UK foreign intelligence service

MoD - Ministry of Defence

NOK - Next of Kin

Op - Observation post

PE - Plastic explosive

PIRA - Provisional IRA

RPG - Rocket propelled grenade

ROE - Rules of Engagement

RTU - Returned or Return to Unit

Remington 870 - Pump-action shotgun

SOCO - Scene of crime officer

SOP - Standard operating procedure

Sig Sauer P226 -    Handgun used by SAS and other military units

Stinger - Shoulder-fired Surface-To Air missile (SAM)

TAB - Tactical Advance to Battle, a long march

Tubes - Mortars

UAV - Unmanned aerial vehicle such as a Predator Drone

# CHAPTER ONE

The assassin entered the covertly fortified cave in the Khost region of Pakistan. From the exterior, the location appeared to be just another gaping hole in the rock face. He began to relax as he ambled casually between his escorts, noticing how clean and organised the cavern appeared. *Something like out of a 007 villain's lair*, he reasoned. The cool air was a welcome relief to the suffocating heat of the arid landscape that sweltered under the dome of cloudless blue outside. His traditionally dressed Arab host sat on a beautifully designed rug about three hundred metres inside the heavily guarded complex. The contract killer had been searched repeatedly since making contact with the Sheikh's entourage near the Pakistan border. His dress code was his customary casual attire of faded jeans, sports sweatshirt and a leather jacket that he took off upon arrival in the unrelenting heat. He had left behind his weapons and personal effects in a Jordanian safe box before boarding a private jet that stopped off briefly in Yemen where more guards boarded the comfortable Gulfstream aircraft for the last leg to Pakistan.

'Welcome, thank you for coming.' The Arab said in perfect English.

'Salaam Alaikum,' the killer replied in adequate Arabic. He knew from the initial internet contact why he was asked to make the trip but he erred towards politeness. 'What can I do for you?'

The Arab looked at his robed Yemeni bodyguards, pondering the difference between them and the man who now sat cross-legged opposite him. All of the Sheikh's close protection detail had been trained by US Navy SEAL instructors as part of a joint Yemen and US anti-terrorist exercise. The reputation did not fit the man whose gaze he met. Yet, there was something in this stranger's cold grey eyes that the Sheikh's men did not possess. Something behind the eyes, disturbing yet intriguing. He handed the assassin a vanilla envelope.

'Can you kill these people for me?'

'Anyone can be eliminated,' he opened the envelope and took out nine A4 photographs attached to nine brief profiles, 'for the right price . . .' the assassin paused, reflecting on what he had just said. 'It's getting away with it that counts to men like me-'

'Men like you? You are one of a kind, or so I was told.' The Sheikh clapped his hands whereupon a guard appeared with a tray containing tea and pastries. Another guard appeared and laid a chrome suitcase beside his employer. 'As per your instructions, half now and half when all of them are dead?'

The assassin did not want to appear perturbed at the nine images so to regain his composure, he accepted a small slice of pastry that looked almond like and asked for bottled water instead of the tea. A generator's hum could be heard further down the cave's interior. The echo of the essential energy supply gave the newcomer a sense of the vastness of the hideout. He had no doubt that the billionaire Saudi prince had more than one of such complexes available for his use when organising meetings as the one that was taking place.

'You are shocked?' The Sheikh enquired, unable to detect any alarm.

'No. Most people have their reasons for people they want killed and I never enquire as to these reasons. But . . .'

The Sheikh eyed the Westerner with suspicion, 'but what, friend?'

'Not that it matters to me but this ninth and final target makes no sense as it would achieve nothing. And, his death if it comes to pass, will put a lifetime target on both of our backs. They will never stop looking for us . . . do you understand that?'

'Of course I do . . . open that case. Please?'

'Sure.'

'Are you not even interested in knowing my identity?'

'No . . . I'm good with "Sheikh" as the only thing that concerns me is your money. This is just business.'

The killer clicked the latch to open the glimmering case and ran his hands along the inner rim. He would check it thoroughly later, if he decided to do the job. 'Twenty five million in diamonds?'

The Saudi interjected. 'The other twenty five million in dollars and pounds, payable into your account on completion of all nine tasks.' He licked a remnant of Basboosa from his fingers. 'So, the twenty five million as promised and another twenty five million when the job is done. Though we will have no need to speak directly again, I will need a temporary cell phone number from you so that my London contact can fulfil your intelligence needs as to the targets' movements.'

'Who is your London contact?'

'A loyal servant, no need to worry who. This task will be accomplished in half the time with the proper intelligence. You will never meet him, just speak to him using one of those throw-away phones.'

The Westerner tried another almond delicacy and changed his mind about the tea. The guard who poured it gave him a curious, if nervous look. He ignored the glance and returned to the photos. He tossed the eight photos on to the magnificently crafted rug, 'he's not a problem . . . his protection are highly trained and courageous but they are mainly for show, let down by interfering agencies combined with the logistics of-'

'Killing a head of state is not a problem?' The Sheikh remarked curiously.

'The first six people will be dangerous enough as they work as a unit. The seventh will have protection but not too difficult. Head of state or not . . . the eight target is fine. As I said, the ninth victim would put me in harm's way and that is not a situation I take lightly. . . even for fifty million.'

'Will you do it?'

'Whenever there are multiple targets, it is far easier to strike when they are all present at the same location. Anything else borders on the insane. This is trickier than I imagined.'

'The unit and their financier have to be taken out first, everything I have planned elsewhere depends on that. Then the eight and . . . the ninth man being the last, in that specific order.'

'It would be my final contract, naturally. I could never work again; it would be foolhardy to even try.'

'Will you do it?' The Arab repeated.

'I need time, maybe a day, to see if this is possible?'

'What about my son?'

'I am not a stupid man, Sheikh. He's safe and will remain safe until I return to Europe intact.'

Before agreeing to meet with the Sheikh, the assassin had demanded insurance that there would not be a trap or rendition awaiting him. Hence, he had hired a retired doctor to meet with the Sheikh's entourage and provide DNA proof of their kinship. The doctor, oblivious to the situation, accepted twenty thousand UK pounds to protect and confine the dubious Saudi teenager in a secluded Swiss setting, sedated most of the time.

'Where will you go while you think on this?' The Sheikh enquired.

'Nowhere . . . I was hoping you would provide a place for me to rest my head?'

'Naturally, it is traditional for us . . . you will be my guest. We might talk about things-'

'Such as?'

'About you! To get an idea of the type of man you are. It is said that you are the only soldier to have served in both British and American special forces?' The killer gave no sign of acknowledgement. 'There is so much speculation and so called mythical talk of you and . . . your reputation. If it is not too intrusive?'

'It is.'

The smile faded from the Arab's face. 'Well, I will tell *you* something if it might interest you?'

'If it pleases you, Sheikh.'

'Bin Laden?'

'He was a puppet . . . a fanatical dreamer living on his reputation.'

'Ha-ha . . . you are well informed then. But, do you know of the man who pulled the puppet's strings?'

'I think I am looking at him!' The assassin showed no emotion, a fact that made everyone uncomfortable.

The Sheikh propped up his silk cushions and stared directly at the assassin. 'I know you say that you never need to know the reasons why your clients seek the elimination of people, but I am going to tell you why I want that ninth man dead!'

'If you insist, I am your guest.'

'I want his mother to feel the pain . . . the heartbreak, the knowledge that she outlived her son.'

'So you are saying that they are responsible for your son's death . . .?'

'My second oldest boy was in a Yemeni training camp two years ago when it was raided by a joint British, American and traitorous Yemen government task force. He was cut down like a dog, so . . . a son for a son!'

'It's your money, Sheikh. One question does spring to mind though and it does not concern the targets.'

'Ask it!'

'Why me . . . an infidel, a Westerner. You have many devoted followers willing to die for the cause?'

'You are the best at what you do, seemingly. I have heard that your motto is "98% preparation and 2% kill" which is a professionalism greatly to be admired but I wanted you mostly because of that crazy Israeli. Anyone capable of doing that and getting away with it . . . is someone to be taken *very* seriously. Yet everyone still believes he died of a stroke? The Jews are a proud race.'

'I have heard that quote was attributed to me and as I said to you, I never comment, but as to your ratios, I would say that 49% preparation, 2% kill and 49% *escape* would be more appropriate. And you are right, the Jews are a proud people and, in my opinion, a fierce enemy to take on. I admire them.'

The Sheikh cleared his throat. 'I will activate my network of cells in the West to cause enough distraction for you to go about your business. They are highly trained and are willing to die for the cause.'

'I act alone. Whatever you do beyond that is none of my affair. It's getting at the last two of these targets in one *situ* that is my concern.'

'You are a curious man, even for an infidel. We will have food at eight this evening?'

'It would be a pleasure, shukran.'

'You know a little of my language, I see?'

'Well, I did spend some time hunting and killing men who spoke it.'

A tall Arab who had been hovering in a nearby shadowed alcove stepped forward. He was the Sheikh's closest homeland bodyguard who had met with the assassin when he landed in Jordan the previous day. Unlike the other guards, he was dressed in an expensive coral blue, white trimmed tracksuit. His rolled-up sleeves revealed a myriad of scars, mostly blade wounds. The warrior carried no AK47 or sidearm; his presence was enough to deter anyone from seeking to harm his benefactor. He was the epitome of the fearsome Mujahedeen, a giant who stood muscular at over six and a half foot tall. He knelt down and whispered in his employer's ear.

'Atmani insists upon staying by your side for the duration of your stay with us, my friend?' The Sheikh remarked through another mouthful of Arabic sweetness. He was the far side of 60 and chubby, a man who appreciated the finest money could buy.

'Not a problem,' the assassin replied flippantly.

'While my son is under your . . . quarantine? I cannot allow you to be within close proximately of guards who are carrying weapons. We are strangers and there is no bond or trust established . . . agreed?'

'Naturally Sheikh . . . only sensible to take every precaution. I would take the same measure myself in your place. Now more importantly . . . what is for dinner?'

The Saudi Sheikh was awoken in the morning to the news that his guest had left, along with the contents of the reward case. It had been left behind, along with the hidden tracking device. Three guards were unconscious and one was missing. Atmani lay outside the cave complex, his neck broken and his jeep missing. There was a note tucked under a rock beside his corpse.

*"The job will be done; all nine subjects will perish as to your instructions. Firstly - the six member unit. Secondly - their backer. Thirdly - the head of state. Lastly - the royal. You will not seek to interfere directly in my actions. You can contact me if needed through our initial channel of communication.*

*We will not meet again unless you are fool enough to withhold the remaining twenty five million balance. I will send confirmation of how the funds are to be distributed to my accounts."*

Sheikh Abdullah ibn Saud, a second cousin to the Saudi Arabian king, screwed up the note as he took in the expanse that dropped away before his morning-heavy eyes. A stream of cauliflower clouds split the vast blue heavens that belittled his vengeful thoughts. The infidel was a professional killer who would see it as a duty to carry out the nine assassinations but then he would be surplus to any and all requirements. There were other dangerous men who had blood ties to the Sheikh. In some ways, even more dangerous, as they cared not for their own lives.

# CHAPTER TWO

*COBRA is an acronym used for emergency meeting government's hierarchy during times of national crisis ana ... incidents affecting Britons abroad. The term derived from urgent gatherings originally held in* **Cabinet Office Briefing Room A.** *It has the power to call upon all affiliated security, intelligence, police and military agencies. As the saying goes - "Whatever Cobra wants, Cobra gets." When all legal and morally acceptable means had been exhausted, the question that was asked was simple - what deniable resources would Cobra use that could be disavowed if exposed?*

**David Keegan** is former 22 SAS Regiment who had been 'returned to unit' and subsequently left the British army at the early age of twenty-nine. Nobody, including his closest friends, knew the real reason why such a dedicated soldier had been 'RTU' by the SAS. The truth was that he refused to use a human shield when targeting a Bosnian war criminal. Besides his 'Killing House' firearms expertise, his use of lethal force in close quarter combat was widely admired. Keegan was formidable in Tai Chi and Aikido but Jujitsu remained his favourite, most fearsome martial art.

**Steve 'Coop' Cooper** is a former SEAL TEAM SIX sniper with a fondness for money and a hatred for anything jihadist. Steve had a particular liking for England and had served alongside British Special Forces on two occasions in

.t Gulf War. His affection for Britain had been fostered in his youth,
.ening to tales of his great grandfather who had married a fair-haired English
nurse after the Second World War. They had met in Devon and fallen
completely in love before his deployment to the Normandy beaches. Cooper, the
oldest member of the unit at forty-four years of age, considered himself an
honorary Englishman.

**Sara Brahms** is a Mossad agent; retired, though it has always been said that
once in, you never leave. Her expertise is intelligence, gathering it and making
sense of it. She had a rumoured IQ of 161 which she denied but did claim to be
a keen observer of body language, a skill embedded into her consciousness in
her early training years, meeting travellers at Ben Gurion Airport where Mossad
placed their raw recruits; their first dealings with foreigners waiting for perusal
in the huge passport control area. Sara had looks and was the youngest of the
group at twenty nine. All of the others had seen how capable she was of extreme
violence but they still looked upon her as a younger sister.

**Yakov Zorin**, 43: a former Spetsnaz interrogator. His role was simple; he made
prisoners talk. "Everybody talks eventually . . . everybody." Other members of
the unit frowned upon his participation but the unit's leader regarded the
Russian as an essential clog in the machine. Officially, he was still in the
employ of the Russian military but his Spetsnaz commanding officer had
refused to treat him as a deserter; instead marking him down as an unsuitable

13

soldier in need of psychiatric care. Zorin hated his homeland; detested the way the military had been treated in the Chechen campaign. Since Putin had replanted the Soviet seed, he hated it even more, vowing never to return.

The final member of the unit is surprising in the fact that he was once a sworn enemy of The United Kingdom and its armed forces. **Seamus Cooney** was at one time the Provisional IRA's most lethal bomb maker. When the Anglo-Irish peace accord was signed, he went to work on his uncle's farm in Maryland. His world changed forever when his pregnant wife was killed on 9/11/2001. He now made bombs again. He was the unit's explosive expert, capable of defusing IED's as well as a genius at their construction and placement. He and Keegan had not much time for one another initially, having been sworn enemies, but their relationship had thawed to the extent that the past was no longer an issue. It got to the stage where Keegan used to jokingly refer to Cooney as "The Irishman" or sometimes just "Irish". Cooney responded in kind by calling Keegan - "English". This banter was now commonplace, something that would have been inconceivable at their initial unit debrief. He had a beautiful Alsatian Shepherd, Rebel, who he spent years training in the art of explosives detection. The dog was more of a friend to him but it had come in handy on two previous occasions, once when the unit had been sent to Egypt during the Arab Spring. Rebel had wandered through the unit's quarters on the outskirts of Cairo one moonless night where he discovered an IED waiting to incinerate anyone in the lounge who switched on the television. Ever since, Cooney's colleagues had grown fond of the animal, except Zorin, who disliked pretty much anything or anybody.

Their commanding officer was a former British SAS Regiment captain, **Kenneth Harris**. He was the most naturally gifted killer of the six-member unit. Many members of the SAS frowned upon their 'Ruperts' (officers who had been fast tracked into the Regiment) but Harris was an exception. He had earned their respect the hard way, leading from the front, wounded twice while saving a sergeant from capture and certain death in the Afghan wastelands. The unit as they all referred to themselves, had just one objective - tradecraft and lethal covert operations for the British government when it could not be seen to sanction its own military, police or intelligence actions due to deniability.

Then one late autumn day, the unit faced their deadliest challenge - an enemy with no face, no name and no past. Not one single intelligence agency could ever get a fix on his location until he once again disappeared into the ether. Some agencies even began to doubt his existence. Harris' unit was well funded with all six set financially for life but the foe they were soon to encounter was in a different league, in the Black Ops sense. He was the most feared contract killer alive due to his reputation for certain kills, and the price he demanded, though more times than often he was offered a larger sum than he thought necessary. The death industry was a lucrative industry. If someone wanted a person or persons assassinated, it could and would be done with the very minimum of collateral damage. If innocents died as a result of his actions, it would be for one reason only - to protect his anonymity. He had his limits in this department such as when a Russian billionaire paid him five million US dollars to kill his wife and make it look like a terrorist attack. The kill was supposed to be aboard a yacht in the Caspian Sea but the yacht turned out to be a floating city with over one hundred and fifty people aboard, including families with small children. The assassin refused the job and returned the Russian's fee, minus ten percent expenses. The Russian was furious and tried to hit back with a daring plan of entrapment. He asked for a 'meet' to renegotiate another time and location for his wife's death. The meeting never took place according to the billionaire's aides as their boss was found hanging from the roof of a barn near his Crimean holiday mansion the night before the meet. His kills were a work of art with every infinitesimal detail scrutinised repeatedly. It would be done and appear to be done by an opposing faction. He never made mistakes.

Harris and his unit, together with his Whitehall and affiliated Langley CIA contact had never had the occasion to seek the man. They remained dubious as to a man who could live such a life and leave no trace in the modern computer age. Unlike 'Carlos The Jackal' and other notorious assassins, the man completed his task and vanished without trace, not to be heard of or suspected of something until after a coup, assassination or something inexplicable had occurred. If he truly did exist and was culpable for any of the surreal hits attributed to him, then his calling card was simple - he left no trace. Intelligence agencies all over the world had coordinated their efforts following a few implausible hits that made no sense; the ones where it turned out that the particular attack was made to look like the work of an enemy but one which the particular enemy took the time and risk to prove it had nothing to do with. In the spring of 2012, an infamous meeting took place in Reykjavik where intelligence officials from the West had met with some peculiar contemporaries; those of China, Pakistan, Iran, Russia and North Korea among other unlikely regimes deemed suitable to cooperate. Three days of 'information sharing' gleaned nothing except that he was probably a male Caucasian in his thirties. There was no need to pass out dossiers at the extraordinary meeting's close; they agreed between them that 'if' he showed up anywhere, they would all be willing to network with the other agencies. The CIA's deputy director laughed aloud as he shook the hand of the sincere looking woman who had represented the South Africans. "What a crock of horseshit," he was heard to say, adding "anyone who catches this ghost will hire the fucker themselves!" The CIA man publically doubted the existence of the assassin insisting his agency had spent too much effort and money in trying to locate a shadow. A series of unsubstantiated and mysterious attacks were merely coincidental and probably the work of a variety of hard-line extremists was what the spooks at Langley had tried to convince their leader on Pennsylvania Avenue in Washington DC. The president at the time concurred with them until one day while playing golf in Texas, he found a blood stained ball in the course's deep rough; his ball. The Secret Service swarmed all over the area and after a fruitless search, they had the blood stained ball examined. The blood belonged to a former SS officer who had been rumoured to be living in Illinois. The ninety two year old German had been accused of causing the deaths of hundreds of Jews from the Warsaw ghetto of 1941. In truth, an Israeli internet millionaire had paid two million dollars to kill him. His corpse was eventually found near a synagogue in Chicago; he had died from an overdose of gas asphyxiation. The papers later printed a story that claimed that the US State department had allowed the suspected war criminal to live in the United States after offering up Nazi files on Russian atomic engineers. The golf ball was disposed of by a White House secretary despite requests by the Secret Service to hold it for further investigations. The unspoken reality of the Reykjavik meeting was an underlying consensus - no smoke without fire. An anonymous assassin was out there and more than one government would gladly pay for his services while others would detain him and melt the key in the lock.

## CHAPTER THREE

New Road, Harlington, Middlesex. A three-man sleeper terror cell in the pay of the Saudi Sheikh had scaled a three-tier apartment block in the guise of roofers. They had waited most of the morning and mid afternoon, their eyes trained on Heathrow Airport's northern runway that lay within a mile of their position. Each man lay under a lightweight decorator's canvas, their RPGs (Rocket Propelled Grenade) waiting for their target. Their fellow cell, a suicide-vested trio waited in the crowded arrivals hall of Terminal 3. Though air conditioned and well maintained, the area was always a mass of sweaty, eager bodies when awaiting the arrival of the big jets from The United States. Said, the leader of the cell looked up at the arrivals board to see that the 747 due to land from Newark was on time. All he waited for was the noise of the explosion from the runway. It came ten minutes later when two of the three RPGs struck the American Airlines A319 as its wheels scattered the afternoon shadow of the distant sun. One missile hit just above the wing, the other, just yards away near the tail fin. The third RPG flew through the blazing vacuum to land in a distant field. One hundred and sixty eight souls perished in an instant with burning wreckage and parts causing more fatalities in nearby structures. The explosion rocked the floors of the neighbouring terminals. Said gathered his breath and looked around to find his fellow martyrs in predestined positions. All three closed their eyes and detonated their vests after loud acclamations of their god.

The simultaneous blasts ripped the arrivals hall apart as body parts collided in mid-air, seconds after the initial flash. The blasted walls and askew pillars within were covered blood red as the screaming began and debris started to fall. Among the two hundred causalities were seventeen children; youngsters standing beside their parents awaiting the arrival of their American friends, families and assorted guests.

\*\*\*

An emergency meeting of Cobra was scheduled within minutes of the breaking Heathrow news. The Prime Minister had been in Cornwall and was flying back to London. The Home Secretary, the Defence Secretary, the Metropolitan Police Commissioner along with representatives of the intelligence and military would be waiting for him in Downing Street. British airspace was closed indefinitely with incoming flights diverted to reachable European cities. All public transport was suspended and stations evacuated.

\*\*\*

The Sheikh, reunited with his teenage son in his opulent Riyadh palace, watched as Al Jazeera devoted all their attention to the UK atrocities. His smile widened hours later when the laundry van exploded beneath New York's Times Square Marriot Hotel killing eighty nine people and then he beamed as five more of his martyrs caused the death of seventy shoppers in a Riyadh shopping mall. A cool breeze wafted through the lace curtains of the spacious, ornately decorated lounge, adding a sense of contentment to his already triumphant demeanour. His martyrs had killed Westerners and Saudis alike; indiscriminately spraying the crowds before detonating their vests as the emergency services arrived. He ate his favoured pastries, knowing the worst was yet to come. It would not rival 9/11 but it would cause the same fall out - the possibility of war. A situation he would use to eliminate his rivals and claim the Saudi crown from his cousins. His homeland terror cell was waiting to strike at the very heart of Saudi power; his empowered cousins.

\*\*\*

The occupants of the lone aircraft in UK airspace were reeling with shock as the events unfolded. The Prime Minster drifted away from his entourage and asked to be left alone in the rear of the jet. He glanced out at the sleeping clouds, wondering what else was coming. How would his predecessors have handled the situation? Was there going to be more war, more body bags?

\*\*\*

'Target acquired,' Cooper whispered into the communication comm attached to his jacket collar. As the **"engage"** signal came back, he placed his index finger on the trigger and squeezed. The high calibre 7.62 round pierced the windowpane and exploded within the head of Jak Shulku, the Albanian bodyguard and brother of a man renowned for kidnapping innocent teenage girls and pimping their drugged bodies to his native Balkan friends and associates. The three other men sitting at the card table had hardly time to react before the front and back doors of their improvised brothel burst open through the use of shotguns. Two figures in casual fatigues pointed their weapons at the startled Albanian trio.

'Where is Ardit?'

'Who . . . who Ardit?' A heavyset card player asked.

He was shot through the forehead.

'Where is Ardit Shulku?' David Keegan, the former SAS trooper asked the two remaining gang members.

'He is in the Albion House car park talking to a girl.'

'The car registration?' Asked Seamus Cooney.

'Ardit 47 . . . it's his personal plate.'

As he finished his sentence, he hit the rear wall, courtesy of a pump action trigger. His colleague met a similar fate a second later.

The unit leader spoke into his collar comm - 'Albion pub car park with a female, registration - Alpha, Romeo, Delta, Indigo, Tango, 4, 7 . . . copy?'

**'Roger that . . . target in sight.'** Steve 'Coop' Cooper responded, adjusting his sight. The round from his MK11 shattered the engine block of the silver Bentley.

Ardit Shulku felt the force of the blast as his car bonnet flew into the sky. The teenage waitress beside him screamed in panic, as did Ardit when he saw two men approach his immobile vehicle.

'Out . . . get out with your hands on your head!' Keegan shouted as Sara Brahms provided cover with Cooney bringing up the rear.

Ardit thought of reaching for his waistline pistol when another round cracked open his windscreen. 'Okay . . . okay,' he bellowed, hoping to draw attention from a passerby.

'Look at my eyes scumbag . . . look into my eyes . . .' Keegan shouted.

'Okay . . . okay!' Ardit screamed in panic, spittle dripping onto his red silk shirt.

'Take your eyes off mine and I will shoot you dead . . . understand?'

'Yes . . . okay.' The terrified Albanian kept his stare on the man pointing a shotgun at him.

Two hours passed during which the once fearsome gangland kingpin dwelled upon his past. He had been taped from head to toe and transported from vehicle to vehicle. He had no idea where he was or who his abductors might be. He soon found out.

The space sounded hollow and he had a hood over his head. *This was good; they did not want me to identify them so I might be let loose?*

The next words spoken shattered his illusions.

'You must know that you are a dead man, Ardit?' Kenneth Harris remarked casually as his unit stood around the mirror walled interrogation room, all privy to their prisoner's pervading sense of dread. The ominous scent of fear.

The Albanian shook his hooded head in despair.

'It's just a question of how you want to die . . . nothing else should disturb your thoughts. We just need the location of a certain individual-'

'If you are talking about Simchuk you can forget it because even if you torture me, I won't reveal anything. He would find out and slaughter my children, my entire family.'

'Very well Ardit . . . let us proceed with the messy killing of you part.' The ex SAS captain said in an unusually cheerful tone. 'My Russian colleague here would normally peel off your skin but he has something far uglier in mind. It's actually quite sickening to even hear him speak of it. All righty then?'

'You can't do this . . . it's inhuman . . . against the law to torture-'

'Ah . . . there you have it Ardit! You see, we don't operate within any law. You won't hear of any Geneva Convention protocol around here.'

The Albanian soiled himself.

'How are you with cats Ardit?'

'Cats?'

'Not your household pussy so to speak . . . I mean the larger ones that rip a man to pieces and eat him while he is still breathing?'

'Please . . . you have to understand! Simchuk is the devil! He is a demon responsible for hundreds, maybe thousands of terrible things. He operates all over Europe?'

'That's exactly why we want him Ardit . . . you are just unfortunate in that you will have to tell us everything about him.' Harris replied sensing his mobile's vibration in his trouser pocket.

'Cats?' The Albanian enquired again. 'What are you going to do?'

'I am going to do nothing myself, we have more important issues as there are people out there who think it is alright to blow up our airports. I will leave you in the capable hands of our Russian friend. You are going to tell him Simchuk's exact location and what to expect there.'

'No-no-no . . . I can't!'

'I beg to differ,' the giant Russian responded as he grabbed his subject by his constraints.

The other unit members looked at Harris who gave his customary shrug of the shoulders as if to say - *any of you want to torture someone?*

The unit had use of a communal base; a sprawling mansion set back off the A40 Motorway near a small Oxfordshire town. The property was owned and sublet by one of Britain's wealthiest men, a friend of Kenneth Harris. He was a man who made his vast fortune building a transport and telecommunication empire out of outlandish publicity stunts. He sat in the House of Lords. Harris and he met very rarely but they shared the same belief - Britain was going down the toilet and something had to be done. The mansion and grounds had been modified years before with a warren of tunnels running beneath the extensive estate, a series of escape routes for any unit members who found their backs to the wall. There was a helipad above the stables but this was purely a decoy whilst the unit escaped beneath the tunnelled maze of subterranean escape routes below. At the entrance to each tunnelled exit were regularly maintained mountain bikes. At the end of these tunnels were innocuous exits that would not raise an eyebrow from unsuspecting curious locals. They were rusted gates covering camouflaged tunnel exits, waiting for any use of emergency. The underground labyrinth had been quietly constructed by a force of foreign workers who had returned to the Balkans years before. There were no loose ends. The property was owned and sublet by an offshore company that would take decades to link to Sir Raymond Blanch, a friend of The Prince of Wales. Sir Raymond and former SAS captain Kenneth Harris had met at the Wimbledon tennis tournament years before, quite by chance. They soon discovered they shared a bond of undeniable trust - Britain had not fought two world wars for nothing. Their country could not submit to foreign laws with their liberal immigrant dogma. Kenneth Harris and Sir Raymond Blanch were born to the same caste but their worlds separated when the former became a soldier and Blanch discovered he had a flair for money and marketing. Still, they were as close as brothers. This friendship was kept private to both men. Blanch had discreetly used his influence with the Royal family to make a connection and subsequently, down the line, Harris and his unit became known to the civil servants in power who passed on a discreet word to the particular government in power at any given time. David Keegan, Seamus Cooney, Yakov Zorin, Steve Cooper, Sara Brahms and Kenneth Harris never referred to themselves as 'The Cobra Denial' unit or any other such dramatic term but they most definitely were in the mind of Sir Raymond and his influential government contacts; those privy to the secret. Its public exposure would have devastating implications.

\*\*\*

The mood within 10 Downing Street reflected the gloom outside where a light drizzle had steadily turned into a downpour.

'What about your dogs of war?' The Prime Minister asked the debonair man in a Savile Row suit. Not everyone at the smooth, lengthy table with its twenty high back leather chairs knew of the man's exact identity. A few of those gathered in the low ceilinged room knew he had been in military intelligence and now occupied an insignificant training post at the Foreign and Commonwealth Office but they were unclear as to his precise position among the elected gathering. He was nearing seventy and had the look of a suave character from an American soap opera. His grey, slicked back hair fitted with his modest tan, though in years past his tan had been a lot more pronounced. He had aided the SAS in Oman and had seen much of Britain's military campaigns over the years. Yet he was a civil servant and had briefed Prime Ministers since 1990 when he retired from active intel duty. He had sat in on most Cobra meetings since then as his wisdom and reasoning had often been a mitigating factor. Politicians come and go, but civil servants collect their cheques on time until pushed out to graze.

'Finalising the Albanian affair, sir?' The former spook replied. 'They are on alert and will be heading to Yorkshire.'

'The July 2005 Arab?'

'Yes, Prime Minister.' The civil servant looked around the table. 'As you all probably know he was on our radar for quite some time after the 7/7 bombings but his acquisition is now highly pertinent in view of what has happened at Heathrow.'

The Chief of the Defence Staff, Britain's top military officer, put down his glass of water and readied himself for the continual strife when dealing with the controversial "denial unit" that he himself considered unnecessary.

'I am sick to death of these individuals. They are nothing but callous killers,' the Defence Secretary grumbled. 'Heathrow was an attack on British society, hence, we use legitimate British force to deal with the terrorists who attacked our country today!'

The room fell silent for a brief period before the PM arose from the head of the table and walked slowly to his Defence Secretary who swivelled to face him. The PM let out a deep sigh before he spoke.

'We will use everything at our disposal, but listen to me carefully . . . what happened at the airport today was an outrageous act of unparalleled barbarism on our soil. I will use any and *every* means to catch and punish anyone who had anything remotely to do with it. Understood?'

The MI5 director leant forward with an update. 'We have some mobile footage of the Heathrow attacks and my guess is that the aircraft's black box will provide nothing as witnesses saw projectiles strike it as it landed. Three men were seen leaving the area in a Volvo after emerging from an apartment block-'

'The northern runway has a corrugated grey fence shielding that area if I recall?'

'Yes Home Secretary, it does, but the cell seems to have used the three tier building's roof that gave them an advantage.'

'Always the fucking same, we learn *after* the facts. Every time these lunatics succeed we ask ourselves how we did not see it coming and only then attend to our negligence.'

'Any news of this three man cell?' The PM demanded.

'They most probably escaped through Harlington and joined the M4 heading east, sir. We are using CCTV but Harlington and its back streets do not have many cameras, crazy considering its proximity to Heathrow.'

'Towards central London?' The Deputy Prime Minister enquired.

'It would be my guess,' the Saville Row suit replied, without looking directly at the man he disliked and saw no reason for being in attendance. The present government was a coalition of convenience to his mind.

'Fuck me! This is what our era has come to people . . . waiting. Waiting for these fucks to devise new ways to surprise us.'

All present looked at their leader; none had ever seen him quite so enraged.

## CHAPTER FOUR

Steve Ingram was an unassuming analyst working for Britain's MI6 intelligence agency. He had been designated a mere dogsbody by the recruiter who contacted him after he passed out from Oxford University. Steve was a wardrobe homosexual whose only companion was a Siamese cat named Pearl. His only vice were gay chat rooms on the internet that he accessed from a second-hand laptop that he had bought with cash through a local newspaper advertisement. Occasionally, he would venture out to a Soho bar or one of the gay dance clubs near Vauxhall Cross. Steve carried his official work home with him, in his brain. Ingram was no dogsbody; he had a knack for thinking outside the box, back in the box and around the box. The lowly MI6 slave was a gem - a gem undiscovered. He would spend endless hours on his work computer only to return to his modest semi-detached house to do the same with classical music softly playing in the background. He avoided television and cooked a variety of Spaghetti Bolognaise dishes four to five nights per week. During the initial search for 'the unknown assassin', his mind had wandered beyond the known parameters of intelligence gathering. This man had lived; Ingram was certain of that, as he did not believe in coincidences. But, how did this man disappear in an instant? With that in mind, the civil servant had taken a secure MI6 disc home and after transferring it to his personal computer via a decryption process, he had devised a specific programme. Who had served in the intelligence or military communities and had died in non-combat scenarios over the last 5-10 years? After the Reykjavik intel conference between nations, he began to wither down a list of possible candidates. In other words - were the death reports reliable from civilian authorities? After a chance flirtation with a handsome American in a Victoria wine bar, Steve Ingram came across a name that struck his analytical mind as odd. He was no fool and had been aware that the coffee drinker was probably CIA by the way he was asking unusual questions and making it obvious that he was. The stranger was pointing him somewhere, talking of The Day of The Jackal movie and asking if such a character could exist in reality. The elusive man whose entire portfolio seemed odd to Steve had served with the elite US Rangers and had then easily completed the dreaded SAS selection course only to dismiss the elite British regiment as "highly effective, but too eager". US and UK Special Forces often cooperated in training courses; adapting and learning from each other in the process. He had complained that the infamous mountain slogs had been too easy but most of all, he had a gripe with the SAS 'interrogation' exercise. "How could it be justified when the subject being grilled knew that he was never in any real danger, unlike capture by a genuine enemy?" He had taken part in the legendary Task Force Black deployment in Iraq between 2005 and 2008 - a joint US and UK Special Forces operation against Taleban insurgency. This unusual soldier was eventually medically discharged from the Rangers though it was not clear if he had actually served under Delta Force or SEAL command at any time. Alternatively, had he been SAS all along? It was a tangled web of misdirection, from beginning to end. Files had been lost or corrupted and that is what made it so suspicious. Who could do something like that? A hacker . . . a very pricey hacker? Strangest of all were his service photos. His US Fort Benning file showed a young fresh-faced soldier who you would see in a recruitment campaign. However, his UK Hereford file showed a different man completely - ragged and dead eyed. It was not only the difference in years; it appeared to be a different man. There was nothing more about him after discharge until he was listed as a missing civilian a few years later in the 2011 Japanese tsunami. What had happened between his discharge and 'alleged' death in the horror of the Asian tidal nightmare? Steve petted his cat beneath its chin that made him purr to both their merriment. He rubbed his eyes and made ready for bed only to hear the creak of the floorboards behind his computer desk.

'Don't move a finger . . . don't touch that keyboard.'

Ingram, a non-combatant, turned slowly around, 'you . . . *it's you*?'

'It's not the milkman.'

'I can't believe this!' The analyst said, flicking back a strand of blond hair and adjusting his thin-rimmed spectacles. 'This is unreal!'

'Who put you on to me?' The Assassin asked.

'Nobody, just my intuition-'

'If you know anything about me, you must be aware that I am ruthless to the point of paranoid with regard to my safekeeping, Mister Ingram.'

'I just *knew* you existed but I was given a shove in the right direction by an American I met in a wine bar.'

'What is his name?'

'I don't know, honestly.'

'Don't lie.'

'I honestly don't know his name and I never saw him again. I am sure he was a CIA spook who deliberately played on my sexuality but again, I don't have any idea why he did it?'

'I believe you.'

'Am I going to die?'

'Yes.'

'How . . . how did you find me?' A tear crept from the corner of Ingram's right eye and his voice began to waver.

'Does it matter now, "SuperSteve69" . . . your chat room alias, as I remember?'

'*Fuck!* You must be "Superman69" in that case . . . you have to be. I recall one night I was chatting online-'

'You were drunk that night I'm guessing Steve, and you typed something about how you would show them all at work how clever you were by finding "an invisible needle in an invisible haystack?" I knew you were looking for me.'

Ingram was slipping into shock. 'But how did you know I worked at MI6 . . . how could you possibly have known that?'

'That's my business.'

'And the gay chat-'

'I followed you and several other likely males from your building on far too many tedious nights. Those awful bars . . . how could you bear that dreadful beat music? You bought me a drink one night in Vauxhall and several weeks later you paid me cash for a second hand laptop?'

'You don't look anything like you did on those two occasions . . . from what I recall. Your appearance is totally-'

'Enough. Sorry about this . . . collateral damage I'm afraid.' The killer said this as he knew it meant the subject would blab to cling a second longer to their life.

'I never told anyone else about you. I swear on my . . .'

'Who else knows what you discovered about me. What is the precise knowledge of me at Six?'

'Zilch . . . nothing, an original thought would be their last thought. They'd die from shock. The idiots can't think for themselves. They are totally in the dark.'

'I believe you, otherwise you wouldn't be doing what you are doing now on your home computer. You showed initiative . . . I'll give you that.'

'Don't kill my cat?'

'What recording devices have you active at the moment? Cameras and such like?'

'Nothing!'

'Hmm . . . hand me the cat.'

'No.' Ingram replied using his worn cardigan to shield his feline friend.

'Hand me the cat now or I shoot you and then I shoot the cat . . . or the reverse.'

Ingram looked at the emotionless face of the world's most elusive assassin. *You exist. I was right all along!* He had the appearance of a Goth, a man with pierced eyebrows and inked skin. His clothes were cheap market leather and his hair was a mess. 'Okay, but please don't hurt him?'

'That depends,' the assassin replied taking the sleepy feline between his gloved hands, one of which held a suppressed automatic.

'Depends?'

'Depends on what you tell me. Are there any devices from here to the boundary of your property that might have recorded me?'

'No!'

The killer tugged at the cat's outstretched paw. The feline instinct turned to survival and retaliated by trying to break free. It did not succeed as the man's grasp had been expecting it. The leather jacket had protected his arm from the claws that reached out to escape.

'Are there any devices from here to the boundary of your property that might identify me?'

Ingram bent forward in his chair, 'you bastard, *you bastard* . . . you cruel bastard. You have *me*, don't hurt my baby anymore-'

'Are there any devices from here to the boundary of your property that might identify me?' The killer grabbed another paw. 'I will tear this cat apart before I kill you-'

'There are hidden motion detector cameras in the hedges . . . they record footage of anyone coming to my door.'

'Where are the discs? Are they on that laptop or your PC . . . is there a hard drive back-up?'

'Yes, yes . . . now please release my baby.'

The killer eventually discovered the entirety of his recorded intrusion and set his plan in motion. It had not been much, just grainy shadows and silhouettes of an inept burglar.

'You could let me go you know . . . you have all the evidence of what I know on that hard disc and I will never breathe a word of this to anyone. What's the harm in letting me live?'

'I find it staggering that you should ask me something like that. I have spent years covering my tracks and believe me it is a tedious, although essential procedure. Yet here you are, a nice guy and all . . . highly intelligent but asking me to do something that is completely alien to me.'

'I didn't mean to insult you but surely there can be an exception where you can trust someone and show some mercy?'

'Would you, if you were in my position?'

'No . . . I mean yes, of course.'

'You died the second you latched onto me-'

'If I'm to die, answer one thing?'

'Go.'

'How did you serve both as a Navy Seal and a 22 SAS soldier? It's unheard of.'

'Not that it matters, but what source did you have for that intel?'

'Dragan Tadic!'

'What about him, he's dead.'

'I know. You are reported to have killed him . . . with a-'

'An IED in his kettle. Three of his fellow rapists went with him.'

'I know all about Tadic and his Serbian war crimes. He supposedly said that a Navy Seal was tracking him but later changed it to a former SAS man hell bent on killing him. Was that you?'

'Tadic believed so.'

'His widow has or had, a saying about you.'

'Do tell.'

'That you nearly died in Bosnia after you went rogue and that the only reason you didn't die was because Satan refused you entry-'

The civil servant's words were cut off by a blow from a table lamp that rendered him unconsciousness. The killer stepped back and began to fill a holdall with anything of value. The laptop and the PC's hard drive were the first to load. He returned to the disc room and placed the table lamp's cord around the neck of Steve Ingram. As he began to squeeze, the analyst stirred and made a vain attempt to halt his imminent death. He died soon afterwards, his feet slowly losing their kick. The killer left by the back door with all the evidence of his intrusion. The scene he left behind looked like a bungled robbery that had escalated into murder.

"Say your name?" Were the last gasped words of Steve Ingram as he had watched his cat limp around the ravaged room.

'No can do Bubba.' The assassin replied as he tightened the cord.

'What difference does it make . . . I'm a dead man!'

'You don't want to know, trust me' The killer replied as he finished him off.

He made his way to an alley over a mile away and placed the holdall into the boot of his car. His skin itched from the temporary tattoo ink and he could not wait to remove the fake Goth clips and the green contact lenses. The optical aids were a necessary requirement but they were the least favourite of all his accessories, especially when using a sniper's rifle. His Bohemian Goth was one of several disguises he had used over the years, slowly becoming an expert in wigs and make-up. He had attended a course in theatre design in South West London when he first settled in England. He prided himself on his chameleon disguises, always carrying a substitute disguise when travelling abroad. He had passports and credit cards to match the alias' appearances. He could enter a country looking like a banker or diplomat and leave the country in the guise of a thrifty backpacker. He knew gunsmiths (private weapon manufacturers) on every continent except Australasia, yet never made one-on-one contact with any of them. He had PO boxes to handle secure shipments, ensuring his anonymity. He was a perfectionist who left nothing to chance; killing was easy, evasion was the true art. Yet his true genius was the form of contact when his services were required. He watched the news and spent time online and it was he who contacted people who might be in need of his expertise. There had only been two exceptions; one of which was the Sheikh who was influential enough to put the word out through shadowy intermediaries that only the best would suffice. He had once heard of a former Egyptian commando who placed an advertisement in the London Times, offering to "eradicate pests" for a price. The man was picked up by a CIA snatch team in conjunction with the Cairo authorities. He was subsequently placed in a secure mental health facility and killed himself soon afterwards. Contacting possible clients in the first place was far safer than people contacting him - as entrapment or worse would follow soon after. And to aid him in the negotiation process, he simply used a predefined code agreed with a prospective client. It was simple and effective, sometimes using text from books such as Moby Dick and other literary classics. 111-7-6-2 was as simple as page 111, line 7, the sixth word and its second letter. The book would be simply 'liked' on a fake Facebook account and its code duly embedded on a separate dating site's message box. It was simple; tedious but safe and anyone trying to break or intercept the code would have to know the book title in advance. Before he set off for one of his two London safe houses, he took Ingram's cat from the holdall and pressed on the joint he had appeared to break. After applying suitable pressure, the cat's pain ceased. He found a house where a garden showed evidence of children's toys. He crept into the garden and placed the animal within a kid's toy-house. For a cold-blooded killer, he had an aversion to inflicting harm on animals or children. His targets were a different story, especially the truly malevolent ones. Soft targets such as Ingram were a regrettable consequence due to the life he led.

"Bubba" was a term for a target that he used when he knew he would kill them on the spot or somewhere down the line. It had an unusual origin for him for different reasons beginning when a casual one-night stand had told him that he looked like the golfer Bubba Watson. He then learned that the athlete was born in Bagdad, Florida, as opposed to the Iraqi capital that was spelt with an "h", but a place where he had seen active service. A former colleague then told him that the golfer's birthday was November 5th in the United Kingdom - Fireworks

Day, which he deemed appropriate considering his profession. He never used the nickname and had not heard it since he left the services and fell off the grid, but he surmised that as he was supposedly a dead man, it was a term he would use when addressing a person who was about to die at his hands. He once asked an Italian psychoanalyst in Naples about its deeper meaning, a question that he regretted asking, as it led to an unavoidable tragedy.

## CHAPTER FIVE

Yakov Zorin manhandled Ardit Shukulu along a yellow painted corridor to a black steel door that led to the extensive basement area of Stanley Hall complete with its labyrinth of tunnels. The thud of the Russian's sturdy military issue boots echoed down the concrete stairs followed by the whimpers of the terrified Albanian. As they progressed along the dour grey hallway, the smell of animal dung increased, causing the Albanian to once again soil his ankle tight jumpsuit. They arrived in an enclosure where they were greeted by the snarls of two caged Bengals, rescued by Sir Raymond from poachers in Bangladesh two years previously. He owned a private zoo in Southern France and had been able to get the animals into Britain via a circumspect animal welfare official at Luton Airport. They were huge beasts, eight feet in length covered in dark vertical stripes. Unlike some tigers in Africa and Asia, these were man-eaters, especially when deprived of food for even the shortest amount of time. They were placed in specially constructed cages that led out into an open-air, high-walled enclosure during the day, when the steel shutters were open. The exterior cavity had been the Mansion's swimming pool in its glory days. Back inside, there were three cages in a row divided by stainless steel bars that could be manoeuvred as the situation demanded. The man-eaters were in the outer pens with the middle presently unoccupied although the remnants of congealed blood on the white tilled floor suggested that something or someone had been a guest in the recent past; all to good effect. Depending on a prisoner's level of cooperation, the dividers could be raised, just enough for a claw to snatch the life from a person or inflict a horrific wound. A claw was as lethal as the jaw if directed at the right angle. A prisoner occupying the middle cage would have to lie directly in the centre and not stir an inch, to avoid a growling roar followed by a giant paw desperate to rip into flesh. It was a truly frightening sight to behold, knowing that a caged prisoner could panic and move to either side only to meet one of two snarling killers. Ardit fainted as he took in the sight, sound and smell of his death chamber.

He was awoken by a jet of freezing water within the space of a few minutes. He looked up to see Sara Brahms staring down at him.

'Tell us what we want to know and this can end in a single bullet Ardit?' She asked, hunkering down. 'Otherwise, my Russian colleague here will let these beasts eat parts of you . . . a limb at a time. It's not a nice way to bow out.'

Ardit was now beyond terror but kept picturing his children and other members of his family. 'I can't do it! He'll do worse to my people . . . he is a bigger monster than your Russian thug!'

Yakov smiled as he prepared the inner cage walls, a pump action Remington 870 at his side. He knew the cage's steel bars were impregnable but he also knew his tiger's taste for humans. He just never took the chance. He had seen what tigers could do to men when he had served in the Chechen War, though he also knew that some victims died from shock before the fatal bites were taken.

\*\*\*

Inside the secure Cobra Suite as some junior civil servants referred to it, the Prime Minister sat at the head of his fatigued panel, his sleeves around his elbows and his eyes bleary within shadowy darkened sockets. Everybody was suffering from sleep deprivation.

'I'm no security expert like some here present,' the PM said with a yawn. 'But, I do know that before we can punish these lunatics, we have to have our best people out there looking for them.'

The MI6 and MI5 heads went to speak as one but were cut off as the PM continued, 'you intel guys will carry on with your GCHQ snooping and all your other activities but I think we need something else?' He gave his senior police officer a knowing glance.

The room stayed silent as waiting a revelation.

'Good old fashioned police work gentlemen! Commissioner?'

'Yes sir?' The Commissioner of the London Police Service raised his gaze to meet his elected superior. He too was weary; his tunic was draped over the back of his chair and his tie was undone around his sagging neck.

'Who would you use to trace a fugitive, Commissioner?'

The policeman answered swiftly, 'we have a number of specialist officers who-'

The PM held up his hand, 'no . . . let me put it another way. If someone had abducted your daughter, who would you put on the case?'

'DCI Maurice Peters . . . without a doubt!'

'What about your Detective Brannigan chap . . . he gets results!' The Defence Secretary suggested.

'He is currently suspended Minister,' the officer replied.

The Prime Minister threw his pen onto the table in frustration. 'Well then you bloody well unsuspend him! Get those two men together and send them both after these fanatics. What is wrong with you people! Heathrow, New York . . . not to mention Riyadh. We are at war with scum who want to do away with our way of life!'

The suite was becoming tenser by the hour. The assorted officials had never thought of their leader as a 'man of action' type figure before. The Secretary of Defence looked at his superior and fretted, he was yielding under the pressure.

\*\*\*

Roughly two hundred miles north of the capital lay the sleepy village of Oakworth in West Yorkshire. Inside a pleasant two-up two-down house, a couple made ready for bed. It was late for them but they had fallen asleep during the ongoing late night television news broadcast and had shared a late snack. A Ford Galaxy pulled up down the road from the house and its two occupants joined Sara Brahms and the unit leader in the other smaller vehicle. David Keegan and Seamus Cooney readied their weapons - two Browning Hi-Power 9 mm semi-automatics, complete with silencers and a single taser gun. Keegan was dressed casually in jeans and a hooded top. Cooney wore the uniform of a West Yorkshire Police officer. Harris dialled a number and asked for confirmation.

'It's a go.' He motioned after a short silence.

The former SAS trooper and the onetime IRA bomber checked their comm earpieces, batteries and plastic strips and then slipped out into the night. The air was clingy damp and the hanging moon looked as if it were a luminous bulb in a murky pond.

Keegan prepared to go live but hesitated. 'Do you have any doubts about what we are about to do and what lies ahead in the future, Irishman?'

'None, English! Do you have any doubts?'

'Nah, not one mate. I mean . . . look at this scumbag we're about to meet?'

They clicked their comm units to go live knowing the rest of the team would then hear any further banter.

'Do you know that when it rains, people say it's God's tears, English?'

'What people?'

'Just people Keegan, people in the know. People who wouldn't associate themselves with the likes of you.'

'You Irish wanker . . . anyone ever tell you that you look good in uniform.' Keegan remarked as they walked the short distance.

'Yeah, your ex wife used to say that all the time when I was in Derry, while you were out on patrol. She demanded that I had to dress up in your soldier boy outfit when I was doing her.'

'In your dreams Cooney . . . she's a fuck but she wouldn't have gone near the likes of you.'

'Are you ready, English?'

His comrade nodded and the men separated. Cooney covered his tufts of short brown hair with the peaked officer's cap. Keegan's hood hid his permanently shaven head.

Cooney approached the front door of the target's house while Keegan scaled the rear garden wall and deactivated the kitchen door's lock.

Oakworth was known for the fact that Sir Issac Holden, who invented the 'Lucifer Match' had once lived in its historic Holden House that was eventually gutted by fire in 1907. The unit's target was a man responsible for setting a part of London alight years earlier. Whether he had anything to do with Heathrow was something they would have to find out.

'Who can that be at this hour of the morning?' Mrs Assaf asked as she helped her husband into their Queen sized bed before making her way downstairs.

Moments later, the two intruders pulled the Pakistani born woman into the bedroom. David Keegan pointed his Browning at her head.

'This doesn't happen in a democracy . . . my husband is innocent-'

'What do you know about democracy?' Cooney remarked as he looked about the tidy bedroom.

'Surely an Englishman would not kill an innocent woman?'

'Not normally love, it's not something we do but please don't insult us by insinuating that you knew nothing of your husband's activities. And by the way, I'm Irish, that fucker there is English, unfortunately.'

Smiling, Keegan kept his weapon on the man who sat up in bed in a state of bewilderment. The elderly man had a shaggy grey beard that reminded them of bin Laden. He was shortly tasered and his hands placed into the plastic cuffs before Cooney dragged him effortlessly onto his shoulder and stood up.

'My husband is innocent and poorly. I am a woman and completely innocent-'

'Your husband killed women as well as men. They were all innocent and random. Close your eyes lady.' Keegan ordered.

'Wait, I have to-'

He shot her through the heart and then standing over her corpse, he put another round into her brain and holstered his weapon to his leg's harness.   As they left the bedroom, they heard a noise and were suddenly confronted by a burly youth who had dropped down from the attic's hatch. He swung a vicious punch at Keegan who ducked and pivoted around to crash his elbow into the man's jaw.

'Sneaky Arab fuck!' Keegan observed, pulling out his Browning. 'I'd love to stay and dance as its been terrific meeting you, truly. But time is a wasting so, off you go to those Disneyland virgins pal.' The former SAS man shot the bodyguard in the forehead as he struggled to get up.

* * *

Dazed and hooded, Haroon Rashid Assaf heard the hum of the engine and the acceleration as his transport moved away. He was certain that he had been switched at least twice into waiting vehicles. There were different voices each time and different roads. A motorway, then a turn-off, a back road and then a roundabout. *Whoever these people were, they were going to a lot of effort not to be tracked or caught on CCTV.* Assaf's assumptions were correct. The four-member snatch team had used cars, stolen on the night, and then parked off various junctions and A roads. All the stolen cars would be wiped clean and then abandoned in relay as the unit travelled south. It was tedious and time consuming but it was a safer option than using stolen plates or burning out the vehicles that would attract attention. Anything belonging to a unit member would never be used on a motorway even though their private vehicles were registered to each man's alias. Assaf tugged at his constraints as he pondered the notion of jumping from his transport as it slowed or entered a roundabout. He was not sure who these people were but one thing was clear, they were not official.

# CHAPTER SIX

In a vast industrial complex near the Saudi Arabian King Khalid air force base, the Sheikh met with his most lethal homeland warriors - two pilots attached to 18 Squadron; two fanatics who flew Eurofighter Typhoons equipped with gravity bombs.

'Are you ready to serve me, brothers?' He asked catching his robe as the wind buffeted the small group.

'We are ready to die for the cause, Highness!' Both men replied in unison.

The West had supplied the Eurofighters and the pilots were loyal to only one man; one they believed would set Saudi Arabia free to take its rightful place at the world's banqueting table. For too long, their country had been denied a position of influence and power, due to the ineffective Saud royals who measured wealth in newer palaces and more extravagant luxuries. The Sheikh was their mentor; the only man worthy to govern out of all the Saud monarchy.

The prince eyed his devoted followers with pride. Suicide vests and automatic weapons were one thing - gravity bombs would bring about carnage, carnage at a funeral where most of the Saud clan would be attending, except for himself, naturally. Then, and only then could the coup d'état take place. The Sheikh eyed his deadly exponents of covert terror and sounded his familiar rallying call.

'The West has tanks and planes but we have the oil that feeds them! For too long my royal cousins have been subservient to the infidel. That will change once I control our sacred soil. We will be calling the shots then.'

\*\*\*

Haroon Rashid Assaf sat confined to an interrogation chair deep below a morning sky that he would never see again. His hood was pulled from his head by Yakov Zorin.

Kenneth Harris was the first to speak.

'Welcome to Stanley Hall, Mister Assaf.'

The prisoner blinked repeatedly but stayed silent, trying to ascertain how many of these people there were. Sara Brahms walked forward.

'You are here to answer for your crimes, Mister Assaf. Your wife is dead.'

The frightened captive showed his first sign of emotion but remained silent for a further hour. The people in the brightly lit room surrounded by a wall of mirrors never touched him, except to offer him water through a straw.

'You know you are going to die here Assaf and your remains will be wiped from the face of the earth. You must know that having seen our faces that we will never allow you to live.' Harris motioned to the fatigued man. 'How you die, is up to you alone.'

'What are my choices, soldier boy?' Assaf finally asked.

'So presumptuous . . . is it that obvious?

'I can always recognise a lackey when I see one.'

Harris shrugged his shoulders. 'As I was saying, this is about *how* you die. A mere second or two to three weeks, depending on how your immune system holds out. Believe me when I tell you that Private Zorin here is a man who enjoys his work.'

'What do you want to know? What knowledge do you think I have is worth all this?' His English was becoming clearer by the syllable.

Sara and Harris pulled up two comfortable chairs, inches away from their prisoner. She brushed an auburn curl back beneath her baseball cap. Undone, her shoulder length hair complemented her olive skin and soft green eyes making Sara Brahms a fascinating woman to behold. She had maintained her trim figure into her late twenties and although not curvy in the glamorous sense, her presence was enough to warrant envious and lustful looks in equal measure.

'Who was behind the Heathrow attacks?'

The man looked perplexed. 'Are you serious, bitch?'

'Yes, we are very serious.' Sara responded though she immediately doubted his involvement.

'Nothing. I know nothing of that!'

Sara nodded to Harris who saw a familiar look in her eyes.

'Okay, we'll return to that later. Meanwhile, we want the names of everyone, besides yourself, who had anything to do with the 7-7 London bombings. Anyone who knew, anyone who made a phone call, bought a rucksack, even looked at a rucksack-'

'You foolish bitch . . . Jewish?' Assaf broke into a laugh as he spoke.

'We know that you masterminded the attacks that killed over fifty innocent people on their way to work that day.'

Assaf began chanting in Arabic. Harris motioned to Zorin.

The giant Russian walked over to the prisoner and after finding a vein, injected him with a sedative. He had seen the signs of hysteria before and the best measure before torture was to calm the subject.

'You people think I planned the July 7th London bombings?'

'We know you did, Assaf. I repeat . . . we *know* you did!'

Assaf knew his fate was sealed and he again began rambling in Arabic.

'You can save your virgins speech for the afterlife scumbag.' Zorin said as he hauled him to his feet.

'Torture me all you want but know this . . . you are a group of mongrel scum. I will never talk and the Sheikh will see you all dead. He will trace my disappearance and find you. And then you will die slower than I am about to.'

'We *know* of your Arab friend Assaf,' Sara bluffed. 'Pakistan and Saudi Arabia are as vile as Iran when it comes to sponsoring and training pond life such as you-'

'He will hunt you down like the infidel dogs that you are!'

After Zorin had carried his prisoner away, Sara spoke her mind to Harris. Cooney and Keegan were on the ground floor monitoring the security cameras and preparing dinner.

'He was telling the truth Kenneth, about Heathrow. Though we know he is guilty as sin of the 2007 attacks, there is one thing that bothers me.'

'The mention of this Sheikh?'

'Tell Zorin not to kill him. He is old and has a weak heart. We are going to have to think this through.' Sara said, remembering the way their prisoner reacted.

Harris scratched his neck's fading scar, a reminder of Iraqi shrapnel. 'I know. I didn't say anything when he mentioned the "Sheikh" as I was waiting for your input. Why didn't you ask him about it?'

'To make him think that we knew of the existence of this Sheikh, that we were aware of him. The Yanks were experts at this in Guantanamo.'

'A bluff?'

'Yes, sir.'

Harris picked up the internal wall telephone. 'Yakov . . . put him in solitary. Keep him away from the cats. Understood?'

After the affirmative reply, Harris walked upstairs with Sara Brahms. 'UBL was always known as "The Sheikh" Sara, so you think that there is some other slug out there who has taken over his mantle?'

'Not sure boss but there was something about the way Assaf said the name . . . I mean the title 'Sheikh', that made me think. He might not know this Arab personally but Assaf does know of somebody who is worth taking note of.'

'Yeah?'

'I'm certain of it . . . the way he said it?'

'Is it worth kicking it back up to Cobra?'

'No sir, not yet. Let me have a few sessions with Assaf alone.'

'Okay, but he never leaves here.    We are going to kill him, whatever.'

'Absolutely boss, 2007 is covered with his prints. The newspapers did how many articles on him?'

'Quite a few as I remember but the government did nothing about it.'

'I know . . . no direct evidence. Sometimes that can be the biggest clue in itself, crazy as it sounds. And to think that he thought he could live out his days in idyllic Yorkshire tended to by his wife.'

They reached the canteen area where Keegan and Cooper were preparing lasagne.

'Leave it to me boss, if he has anything on Heathrow,' Sara remarked, 'I'll get it from him and we won't need Zorin's cats.'

'You don't really like Yakov, do you Sara?'

'As a member of our team he is fine but the man himself is as monstrous as his cats.'

'Yeah, but he is our monster and he does what none of us are capable or willing to do.'

'Would you torture a single man to save a thousand lives, boss?' David Keegan asked overhearing the last few words.

'Yes . . . to save a thousand lives. I would,' Harris replied with some thought.

'To save a hundred . . . no, let's open up the hood here . . . to save ten lives? Would you torture a man to save ten lives, boss?' Cooper asked. "Opening the hood" was Cooper's way of getting straight to the point.

Harris saw where the conversation was leading and cut it short. 'This lasagne has to be better than the last slab of shite you served up Coop.'

'Copy that boss,' Cooney interjected, 'that Tika thing last week left my arsehole thinking it had been hit by an RPG.'

# CHAPTER SEVEN

The Prime Minister entered the Cobra suite having endured a restless five-hour sleep.

'Okay . . . I've had some research done on this Brannigan character. He is a loose cannon but he might be of some use. Meantime, tell me about this DCI Maurice Peters?'

The few people seated at the table who had heard of the officer spoke up.

'He's a freak!'

'He's a genius!'

'He is . . . unusual?'

'Commissioner . . . you worked with him? Tell me about him?'

'Do you recall the serial killer who removed the limbs of the victims, Prime Minister?'

'Yes, yes I do. How could anyone forget it! I remember now . . . that was your Peters chap?'

'Sir,' the Secretary of Defence interrupted. 'Shouldn't we be moving on with things? There is a lot to get through?'

'We are scouring London for this second cell and until we catch them, there are not many "things" to get through.' The PM replied. 'Tell me more about this detective chap, Commissioner. You actually worked with him on that case I now seem to remember. Let's get some fresh coffee in here and tell us about it?'

'Anyone mind if we turn up the air conditioning?' The Chief of the Defence Staff asked, unbuttoning his collar.

No one objected and soon a surge of welcome air wafted around the stale room.

'Detective Chief Inspector Maurice Peters is no ordinary police officer gentlemen.' The Commissioner stated. 'It is kind of freaky but he intuitively knows the solutions to certain crimes. One look into a killer's eyes is all it takes to convince him of their guilt, regardless of the perpetrator's alibi or status.'

A few of the panel sighed in frustration but as the policeman spoke about his eccentric officer, they became engrossed in his methods. The clock ticked on during which the Commissioner spoke without interruption.

Peters was a DCI in Saville Row police station in central London, one of the youngest, most fast-tracked Detective Chief Inspectors since the rank was instituted. He had been earmarked for a higher office on several occasions but refused, as he wanted to be on the ground, solving crimes. He also refused all other offers from the Serious Crime Squad amongst others. Ever since he joined the police service in 2002, he had a near perfect record. He was in his early thirties, a brilliant copper, admired and envied by all who watched him work. There were a few exceptions who thought him lucky or "just plain creepy". A few previous partners scoffed that he had some sort of physic powers but were reluctant to admit it outside their circle of friends.

Maurice Peters always gave orders for no one except the 'first officer on scene' to have access to the crime site, except in emergencies such as further danger to life when armed response officers would take over. For this reason, he never drank alcohol and kept a spare battery for his 24/7 mobile phone. His usual scenario was walking into a bloodstained dwelling and asking everyone else to remain outside for a moment. He would then run through a 'series of connections' of possible suspects. He would inspect the corpse's cause of death and picture every possible scenario - wife, husband, lover, parent, child, sibling, stranger, debt collector, neighbour, bar pick-up, mailman, milkman, anything that sprang to mind from the environment he found himself in. Only then would he allow access to the SOCO (Scene of Crime Officers) team. He pictured himself as the killer and what he would have done, even before he was informed of the victim's identity. He would match the forensic report and victim background to how the killer had entered the victim's domicile. He would then retrace the victim's movements as far back until he came upon something that 'clicked' in his mind. He often spent countless, unpaid hours revisiting crime scenes. He would watch a suspect's house for any irregular activities, as he knew that once a human takes another life, they change - it is impossible to stay the same.

On the 4th of July 2010, his skills were put to the sternest of tests. A young American law student by the name of Maureen Walters had been found butchered in the front garden of the house she shared with three friends in Crystal Palace, South East London. The crime was shocking due to its extraordinary brutality. Peters led the investigation but after three fruitless months, only one possible lead had been established and it was tenuous at best. Walters was last seen in Central London's Leicester Square after leaving a July 4th celebration party attended by hundreds of fellow American revellers. The law student had been ripped apart by someone who then unsuccessfully tried to remove her head. On the last day of the month - July 31, the killer struck again. The mangled body of a headless female was found in London's Regents Park. Through tedious and methodical searching of CCTV footage for a certain type of van, a suspect was named, one Abah Obunike, a London plumber of Nigerian origin. Namely, the Igbo people who had a history of head hunting. Peters thought otherwise even though everything pointed to the African. He had a theory that the killer was a woman, envious of other women. A bin woman or something similar who worked in a predominately male environment. Probably the butt of jokes and possibly associated with Abah Obunike in some way. Abah Obunike was questioned and named a Belinda Miller. He had fixed her neighbour's toilet flush one night at a party that he attended. Miller, being the woman's neighbour was present. He claimed she had a deep hatred for attractive women. Belinda Miller's Stratford home was searched for a week and a day. The surrounding grounds and gutters were picked through by a relentless team of experts who found nothing incriminating. The case went cold. Peters was working on an assault case six months later when a call came through that a mutilated corpse had been found in the Thames just behind Tower Bridge. It was a young student whose arms had been cut off. The serial killer was back. An hour later, a young woman was just discovered in the water near Hammersmith Bridge, minus her legs. The serial killer was collecting body parts. Peters was on the scene when the second body was discovered and worked out that the killings had taken place in the Richmond area, further up river. As he and the Commissioner himself raced along the Embankment, they had a near accident with an ambulance coming the other way.

Ten minutes later, the ambulance found its path blocked outside the Causton Street Ambulance Station. The driver got out when ordered and knelt down with her hands behind her head. It was Belinda Miller and even though her ambulance carried an icebox, nothing incriminating was found. Once again, despite the early morning coincidence, Miller walked free. A colleague of Peters', Sergeant Lauren Friars was butchered a week later. Her torso was missing; her remains found near the Docklands doorstep of DCI Maurice Peters.

It was a classic set up; the killer was taunting the police, and getting away with it. Four months passed after which DCI Peters found himself wrapped up in another unrelated case but Miller was still very much in his thoughts, every waking hour. He had personally followed her nearly every evening since the Friars murder. She changed jobs and basically kept her own company. Then, one balmy Friday afternoon, Peters received a call from a councillor who represented the people of Richmond. Maurice had requested numerous activity reports from a variety of West London authorities. The DCI was certain of one thing, the river Thames body parts were hidden somewhere in Richmond, probably on ice. He was sitting outside Miller's house when the call came through. Councillor Ritchie had rung to say that a woman of Australian origin had caused a fuss over the proposed redevelopment of a riverside gardening allotment in Richmond. When the next discussion was scheduled, Peters borrowed his neighbour's London Taxi and followed Belinda Miler to her council meeting and sat at the back of the large, crowded hall. When the motion for the planning application came up, an Australian sounding woman objected vehemently, asking people to join her distain. Only one person bothered to join her crusade. Her objection was duly noted but her motion was overwhelmingly denied. Furious, Belinda Miller drove to lot 14 A of the allotment she had purchased ten years previously. Peters followed at a discreet distance and watched as she used a shovel to unearth a small piece of earth. To his surprise, she vanished from sight. Unarmed, as was his way, he crept towards her secret in the darkness. As he drew near, he heard her foul language. Her Australian twang had disappeared, replaced by a harsh London accent. Peters soon found himself at her lair, which was lit up by a wooden staircase that led beneath the ground. He descended as carefully as he could, the only sound being the flights from Heathrow Airport overhead. Breathlessly, he reached a crypt where to his horror; he saw countless body parts in liquid transparent containers. There were arms, legs and heads in a soup like substance, horrifically graphic to the human eye. Belinda Miller received a thirty-year sentence with the recommendation that she never be set free. Peters was like a dog with a bone; if you were guilty, he would catch you.

The Cobra members let out a collective sigh when the Commissioner had finished speaking.

'Get Peters down here.' The Prime Minister affirmed as he arose to go to the bathroom.

'What about Brannigan?' The Commissioner enquired.

'Get him too! I want everyone in on this, not just our intelligence services. We are in deep shit and we need anything and everything that can or could help.'

'Aren't we forgetting the unit, sir?' The MI6 head said. 'These two officers will surely suspect something if the unit compromises us in any way?'

'I agree Prime Minister . . . lest we forget that it was Brannigan who caught that former SAS unit who became the public's "Bad Samaritans" vigilantes back in ninety nine?' The Home Secretary added.

Cobra's boss retook his seat, cursing the amount of coffee he had consumed and his weak bladder that played up under stress. 'A quick summation of Brannigan if you would!'

The Home Secretary opened a file and outlined the main facts, knowing patience was wearing thin all around.

During the 1990's, three former members of Britain's elite SAS Regiment carried out a series of brutal reprisals against career criminals who manipulated the UK judiciary. Paedophiles, terrorists, drug barons and other miscreants were eliminated in a campaign that became infamous as 'The Bad Samaritans' vigilante killings in the media. The tabloid label had gained infamy due to one of the three soldiers working as a part time counsellor for The Samaritan Hotline. His name was Joseph Cassidy, a complex individual who along with his two comrades were finally identified and brought to justice by a London detective, DCI Jim Brannigan. Two died and one was imprisoned where he subsequently died of a stroke. The sting in the tail was that Joseph Cassidy had saved Jim Brannigan's life, not once but twice. Once during his youth in the Northern Ireland conflict and lastly, saving Jim again moments before he died.

Former sergeant Joseph Cassidy and his fallen comrades had paid with their lives as they ridded their beloved England of approximately thirty-seven miscreants.

The room descended into silence once again. The PM hesitated as he felt the pressure on his bladder increasing; then he spoke.

'A copper who can catch a vigilante Special Forces unit is someone who I would like to have on our team. Why was he suspended, Commissioner?'

'Two reasons, the more serious being striking an officer, sir!'

'Oh dear . . . who did he strike?'

'That would be me, sir.'

There was a murmur of disbelief around the conference table.

'What . . . why?' The Foreign Secretary enquired incredulously.

'Because I had suspended him in the first place. The Duke was drunk at the time, sir.'

'The Duke?' A member enquired curiously.

'Brannigan's nickname . . . he likes John Wayne movies as well as red wine.'

'And yet you seem to speak fondly of this Duke character, Commissioner?'

'I do Prime Minister. Despite suspending him . . . which was a given, he's old school, sir. He gets the job done and suffers no fools.'

The file was perused again. Brannigan was extremely fit for his age due to taking up boxing. He was now a fifty-three-year-old Detective Chief Inspector and happily married with an eleven-year old son. The family lived in their modest Kentish Town semi-detached home, despite lucrative offers from security firms and gifts from the Japanese and German governments whose ministers he had saved from certain death in The Bad Samaritan attacks of 1999. He preferred the life of a copper who walked-the-walk, solved crimes and protected the public. His career was once again threatened as his tough method of policing had landed him in another spot of bother. A tabloid newspaper editor who he had long shared a mutual dislike for, had set him up. Consequently, Brannigan had been filmed assaulting a man who he found urinating on a soldier's grave.

'A soldier's grave . . . what soldier, Commissioner?'

'Joseph Cassidy . . . the former SAS vigilante who had saved his life twice. Do not forget, Brannigan is a former military policeman. He saw this idiot urinating on a grave-'

'What was Brannigan doing at this Cassidy's grave?' The MI5 representative enquired curiously. 'Ninety nine till now . . . fifteen years after Cassidy's death?'

71

'The Duke places flowers on his grave every so often . . .?'

'This is unbelievable,' remarked the Deputy Prime Minister.

The Commissioner's face reddened. 'You think so Minister? A man saves your life *twice* and you catch an idiot pissing on his grave!'

'Gentlemen . . . get those police officers down here pronto! And for fuck's sake, try to work towards a common consensus. We're all after the same thing . . . to preserve our way of life.'

'But what about our "black unit" Prime Minster . . . how will that fit in with these two?' The Secretary of Defence asked wryly.

His agitated leader picked up Brannigan's file, 'the unit are our back up. If they get to this terrorist cell before our regular authorities, they will get more out of them than we will. That is . . . if we do use them on this. This is very high profile as you know.' He flicked the file across the polished desk at his colleague before heading to the lavatory. 'Have John Fucking Wayne and Columbo here within the hour!'

His colleagues looked startled, as this was an unprecedented measure; two outsiders, underlings, attending a Cobra meeting in the heart of Downing Street. The man in the Savile Row suit, Bernard Jenkins, caught up with the PM as he entered the bathroom.

'Prime Minister? A discreet word if I may?'

'Certainly Bernard.'

'Brannigan and this DCI Peters chap . . . are we to make them aware of Harris and his unit? Are we to mention them at any time if the need arises?'

'Mmn . . . that is a good question. What do you think, Bernard?'

'I know we have to use everything to stop this terrorism but is it wise to let ordinary coppers know of the unit's existence? Think of the repercussions sir . . . when it is all over and we get back to square one?'

'Two things Bernard.'

'Prime Minister?'

'Will we ever get back to square one? In addition, this Peters is no ordinary copper. Wouldn't it be best to pool our resources?'

'I'm not sure, sir. We can't expect Peters or Brannigan to ignore the unit, *the unit that does not exist* . . . if they both should play a significant role in the forthcoming days.'

'On second thoughts, Bernard . . . do you remember my predecessors' reasoning for using Harris and his unit?'

'Yes, sir . . . because the SAS vigilante episode got rid of people who eluded us back then. Better to use someone like that than chase our tails?'

'Ok . . . then they are not to be privy to any mention of Harris or his unit . . . or even the word "consultants", ok? After all, I just couldn't see an honest plod like Brannigan agreeing with our methods.'

'I'll make sure the rest of the members are aware of your ruling, sir.'

'Thank you, Bernard. By the way . . . the Albanians and Assaf? Need I ask?'

Bernard Jenkin's face told all, though he added. 'They are wrapping it up, sir. Harris and his team snatched Haroon Rashid Assaf last night. They shot his wife and are interrogating him now as we speak.'

'Goodness . . . did they have to kill the woman?'

'Their methods sir . . . she would have been burdensome to transport along with her husband and would have had to have been eliminated at some point due to identifying our Task Force Black unit if she ever was at liberty to do so.'

'All very distasteful Bernard!'

'All very necessary Prime Minister.'

'Any word from Raymond Blanch yet?'

'Yes sir, he phoned me earlier. Sir Raymond is of the mind that we should have the unit in London, in a safe-house in Battersea, to have them ready for anything imminent?'

'Does he now! Well, as I have said before, I and my predecessors are grateful to him and that unit for getting us out of the shit . . . and the papers over the years, but *I* will decide if and when we need them active.'

'Yes, of course sir.'

'It's more of a case of good old fashioned detective and intelligence work at the moment Bernard. The action cannot take place until we uncover these lunatics.'

'One thing to consider Prime Minister. The unit does have a former Mossad member in their ranks. According to Harris, she can find a needle in a field of hay.'

'Mmn . . . there is no question of her coming to Downing Street but could this woman come down and do some snooping?'

'On her own?' Bernard asked aghast.

'Yeah.'

'No Prime Minister, they act as a team and will not compromise on that issue.'

'That unit is made up of some extraordinary people. Give me a few hours to mull this over.'

'Yes, Prime Minister.'

'And stop calling me that when we are alone Bernard. I'm just Dave!'

## CHAPTER EIGHT

While Assaf was left to deal with an uncertain death, his captors had been dining three levels above his basement cell. Harris and Sara listened while Keegan, Cooney and Cooper bantered away; Keegan bemoaning the elitism that dominated British society.

'What about that fool on the train last week?' Keegan asked, 'you're not seriously going to tell me that he and his chums are the crème de la crème of Britain?'

*Train?* Sara's ears pricked up and she raised her eyes to Harris who was doing his best to dig out a slice of lasagne after pouring his favourite walnut oil over it to hasten its liberation from the dish.

Cooney's dog, Rebel wandered freely into the kitchen though he too had reservations about the unit's cuisine and stuck to supermarket tinned fare.

Cooney loved to goad Keegan about the British caste system. 'They seemed a bit unruly but I wouldn't say they were "scoundrels" mate?'

'What occurred?' Cooper asked using a toothpick. They all ate their daily fare as fast food deliveries were not permitted to the house. 'What happened on the train . . . trouble?'

Keegan spoke. 'There were a few college boys sitting opposite Cooney and I and when a middle aged bird boarded at Greenwich, the mommy's boys started to give her some stick . . . annoying her-'

'Why?' The American asked.

'She was a little worse for the wear as we say in Ireland,' Cooney replied. 'And her dress had seen better days. She just wanted a kip while travelling.'

Sara kept her eyes on Harris who remained unconcerned.

'I objected to the lout's behaviour and told them to sit down,' Keegan added, crunching his way through his side salad. 'This one geezer tells me that he was "reading English literature" at Eaton or some shithole so I asked him what that meant and did it entitle him to hassle females on trains?'

'And?' Cooper enquired, scratching under Rebel's chin.

Zorin was oblivious, watching the monitors while delving through yesterday's pasta. He figured he would always leave it a day before eating to see if any of the others developed stomach issues from the previous meal. Reheated crap was safer than fresh salmonella. He did not need to watch the monitors, no one did, as there were intruder motion devices of both the most basic and complex design around the grounds and house entrances. The Russian just liked to look.

Keegan took a swig of sparkling mineral water. 'The upper-class wanker told me that he was studying English more or less-'

'And guess what our former SAS colleague says to him in reply?' Cooney said with a grin.

Sara took her eyes off Harris for a second to gaze at her colleague in arms. They all waited Keegan's reply.

The former trooper wiped his mouth with a napkin. 'I informed the geezer that if he and his fellow idiots did not stop interfering with the woman, that he would spend the rest of his life studying how to wipe his arsehole again.'

Everyone laughed especially when Cooney added that he had also told the colleague boys that reading toilet paper was more their score.

Everyone except Sara, who though amused, beckoned to Harris, 'public transport? Why wasn't I informed of this . . . when was it exactly?'

'Apologies Sara,' Harris butted in, 'David asked me for permission to visit his mother in her care home and I told Seamus to go with him.'

Keegan suddenly felt flush. 'I'll add my apologies, Sara. It's my mother, dementia . . . in the Blackheath nursing home. I asked the boss but it slipped my mind to tell you. It won't happen again without your knowledge. I don't think she has long to go by the way she looked at me . . . hardly recognised me. Parkinsons is one fucked up illness.'

Harris stood up feeling a weight in his stomach. 'That it is David, truly cruel and tough to watch but, as Sara has brought it up . . . remember lads, public transport is a rarity for us. Too many cameras, even if you wear your hooded sweatshirts. I take it that you did wear yours and use that route you mentioned, lads?'

Cooney spoke up for himself and Keegan. 'Absolutely boss. The train part way, walked a few clicks to a cab office on Greenwich High and had the driver wait outside while English visited his mum and I took a stroll around the grounds. The driver wasn't the talkative type, rather glad for the fare type. Repeated the same on our return.'

'Good,' announced Sara putting her plate in the sink. 'It's tedious gentlemen but you never know . . . it might be the saving of us.'

'Just one more thing, and it's nothing really . . . about mommy's boy?'

Harris gave Keegan his look. 'Go on, David?'

'I gave him a slap boss, nothing much, just gave him something to reflect on.'

Sara privately fumed, but waited for the inevitable which duly came.

'Any one of us whose behaviour puts us all in harm's way has to pay for it,' Harris said with a frown. 'How much did we deposit into your bank account last month, Keegan?'

'The usual monthly amount I presume boss, twelve grand . . . I haven't checked for a while?'

'Do you know how much is going in this month?'

Keegan awaited the toll of his fine. 'No idea boss, how much?'

'Not a single penny. You will forfeit your month's hard-earned pay for giving a stupid college kid a slap. Would you like to appeal Keegan?'

The trooper cast his mind back two years when Coop had appealed a month's loss of income after the American had wined and dined a local villager and his appeal had cost him a further month's wage - eight weeks in total. 'No boss, I will not be appealing, just reiterating how dumb I was and apologise once more.'

'Carry on lads. Sara, with me!'

Sara followed Harris into the operations room to plan the death of the unsuspecting Albanian, Simchuk. She felt sorry for Keegan and genuinely liked him but she, more than Harris, had maintained that the lower their profile, the less chance of exposure.

'You fucking English wanker, Keegan!' Cooney said with a smirk. 'Twelve grand down the toilet for slapping a yuppie toe-rag!'

'I know Irish, you don't have to rub it in. Fucking stupid!'

'You English and . . . you Irish . . . are all pussy with your slaps. In Russia, men just slap women but they punch, kick or bite other men. Pussies!'

'You don't understand Yakov, in British terminology "a slap" means a dig, you know . . . a punch?'

'Still pussy boys!' The giant Russian bemoaned as he got to his heavily strapped military boots. He liked black, clothes, boots, women, even his crew cut hair had been dyed black. 'I slap both of you together before you have time to blink!'

'In your fucking wet dream Spetsnaz!' Keegan retorted as he faced off the Russian.

The two men ended up wrestling each other to the ground as they grunted and jabbed in equal measure with Rebel attempting to join the merriment.

'Guys!' Sara called out from the hall. 'The skipper wants you all in the Ops room now!'

'Russian pussy!' Keegan remarked as he helped his colleague to his feet.

'At least I am twelve thousand of your pounds richer, SAS man!'

'All for the sake of meeting that fucking wanker on that particular train.'

'I hate fucking buses and trains in this country . . . full of crying babies with mothers who push prams into you as if they drive tank through Chechnya!'

Cooper, Cooney and Keegan turned to look at the ruffled Russian and laughed. They could tell he was eager to go below and check on Haroon Rashid Assaf. The prisoner had been kept in a cell away from the large cats but their recent feeding of the Albanian criminal Ardit Shukulu had filed the basement's corridors with a unique smell. The kind of smell that hastened up your nostrils when entering a zoo. It was not exactly putrid but it did carry an air of menace as it was in a location where it did not belong. Ardit had given up Simchuk's location and security details and Harris had outlined a plan to Sara to take out the major Albanian criminal at large in the UK. Because of the Heathrow terror attacks, Harris was edgy, awaiting news from Jenkins as to when or even if the unit's services were required. Simchuk would depart London and the planet itself via a high calibre bullet courtesy of their former SEAL sniper. Sara, backed up by Keegan and Cooney, would instigate an incident from an OB detail that would draw him out into the open. Simchuk had a passion for greyhound racing and operated a number of bookmaking stalls at various London tracks. He had begun to visit a track almost nightly with his security detail and glamorous entourage, all of them bored rigid with his recent fondness for the sport. He would die at the next race meeting he attended. A bullet in his head would not stop the pimping and dealing as another tattooed subordinate would eventually step forward to fill his shoes, but it would disrupt their operations for the forthcoming future.

## CHAPTER NINE

Detective Chief Inspector Maurice Peters was an unusual man; in thought, word, deed and appearance. Unlike the NCIS cast and most other clichéd television cops, Peters was best described as funny-ugly at worst; passable on a good day. He would wear the same suit and shirt for two to three shifts if he was scoping a suspect. He lived alone in a converted Docklands warehouse apartment. He did not socialise as his unkempt mop of black hair and general drab appearance invariably caused him to refuse invitations from the outset. He frowned upon loud people, stood five feet, seven inches tall and had no living relatives.

Detective Chief Inspector Jim Brannigan was old school. A former military policeman who had escaped death in Northern Ireland and had joined the Metropolitan Police after the First Gulf War. He had seen enough death and had lost his first wife to foul play. Now happily married to a former colleague who had bore him a son, Brannigan showed no signs of slowing up, taking up boxing once more after he introduced his eleven-year-old son to the sport. His status as a 'hit first and ask questions later' copper was near legend in The Met but his reputation would always revolve around his 1999 detection and elimination of a former SAS Regiment trio who had taken the law into their own hands.

Unmarked vehicles arrived outside both officer's stations just before noon. Thirty minutes later, the men were greeted by a Downing Street official who walked them through the door of Number Ten.

'Any idea what this is about, Peters?' Whispered Brannigan as they were led through to a conference room.

Depending on the circumstances and hour, the members of Cobra would meet at random locations, all within earshot of Whitehall.

'No idea Detective Brannigan. How is . . . Teresa?'

'She's good. Gardening and fundraising.'

'She was a good cop.'

'Thanks Peters.'

'Better than you actually. I bet she wears the trousers in your house.'

'She cleans them first, you wanker. You met anyone recently Maurice?'

'Nah, tied to the job, Jim. You know me.'

'Oh yeah! They still calling you Hercule Poirot?'

'No, never. I think the lads still use Columbo . . . or that chap, Monk?'

'Monk? Fuck me . . . with a nickname like that, I'm not surprised birds stay well clear of you. I mean besides your appearance of an unmade brothel bed.'

'Fuck you Jimbo!'

'Same as Maurice, it's good to see you pal.'

Peters displayed a rare smile as he took in his colleague's familiar dapper appearance. The Duke was dressed as he would be for court or a date with his wife - a dark blue suit, clean shave above a crisply ironed white shirt and a coral blue silk tie. Peters wore his customary jeans and leather jacket.

'Detectives?' Announced the Prime Minister of Great Britain as he stood beside the large conference table pouring milk into a Granola fruit bowl. 'Come in and make yourselves at home. You'll recognise most of these gentlemen.'

'The crème de la crème of British authority . . . Sir.' Brannigan offered cheekily but discreetly.

'Quite so Detective Brannigan. Take a seat please, we have much to go over.'

Peters took a leather chair beside his colleague. 'Is this a Cobra affair, Prime Minister . . . Sirs?'

'We must be bloody obvious but we never seem to use that word amongst us, Detective Peters.'

'Brannigan . . . Peters,' the Commissioner remarked in a dry tone. 'You have been summoned here for one reason only and I take it you know what that is?'

Brannigan paused for once and let Peters do his thing. 'I would have thought the Heathrow attacks would be above our pay grade? Work for the intelligence services, I would have guessed. I'm sorry . . . how do we address you all, individually by name or rank?'

'Relax Peters . . . we don't normally stand on ceremony here though the obvious exception is the chair of this meeting, the Prime Minister. Address him as such.'

'Okay gents,' Brannigan said in reply to the Home Secretary. 'What can two coppers do to help?'

'Detection of course!' Remarked the MI6 head who had already taken a dislike to The Duke. 'We have sparse intel on the whereabouts of three members of the same unit that attacked Heathrow's Northern runway. We are using all possible means, every department, to trace these men before they have the opportunity to launch another attack.'

'Or go into sleeper mode-'

'They won't be doing that anytime soon,' Brannigan said, cutting off the Home Secretary.

'And why not?'

Jim left it to Peters. 'Because of their presence at Heathrow, as you indicated Prime Minister?' The PM nodded, leaving Maurice to continue. 'They have not exposed themselves without cause. The terminal explosions would have been enough for any master planner but these three survived? Martyrs die, sir.'

'I agree Prime Minister,' the Commissioner added. 'Three suicide bombers and another to launch the RPG's would have been sufficient. It doesn't take six men for that. Believe it or not but the jihadists value their martyrs. They use them sparingly. One man on that building's roof would have been somewhat noticeable. Three men would be entirely suspicious no matter how well they concealed themselves. And not only that . . . their method of leaving the area, knowing of the CCTV camera on the main routes, leaves me thinking they want us in a cat and mouse situation.'

'Your thoughts detectives?'

Brannigan looked along the table to the tanned Jenkins. 'I know everyone here Sir but I am not familiar with you . . .?'

The Prime Minister cleared his throat as he wiped his mouth with a Number 10 napkin. 'This is Bernard Jenkins gentlemen. He attends these meetings as a consultant attached to the Foreign Office. So, your thoughts please officers?'

As Brannigan and Peters looked over the single sheet dossier in front of them, Jenkins used a remote to activate one of the large plasma screens that covered the entirety of the rear wall, revealing a map of Greater London. As the wall transformed into a high-tech vision, Jenkins looked over to the new arrivals. 'It goes without saying gentlemen that everything and anything discussed at these meetings remains here?' Jim and Maurice expected nothing less and signed an official document placed before them by an aide who had entered the room by an unseen door. Various heads of departments commented on the attacks and the one concrete sighting of the three remaining terrorists leaving Harlington shortly afterwards.

'Well?' The PM asked, glancing at the Commissioner in anticipation of his officer's expertise.

Peters looked at the map's graphics showing the supposed route taken by the terror cell into the heart of London. He looked at Brannigan who sighed and gestured for him to proceed.

'How quickly does this . . . *committee* work? Fast results I'd wager?' Peters surmised.

'Very fast!' The Home Secretary announced turning from the refreshment table. 'Prepare to be astounded detectives. Cobra, as you mentioned, gets whatever it needs . . . instantly.'

'Okay then,' Peters stood up and walked towards the rear dashboard. 'Let's check on every stolen vehicle from predominantly Asian areas up to six hours before the attacks. And, check every single West London cab firm for pick-ups directly after the attacks . . . and finally we need to look at every abandoned vehicle within a five-mile radius of all westbound routes into London. Make sure they check out service stations . . . like the one at Heston.'

'Explain?' Jenkins said earnestly with his hands behind his head.

Brannigan took over. 'Those jihadists were not headed for Central London gentlemen. From what I saw on television the M4 motorway was at a standstill both east and west immediately afterwards so they wouldn't take a chance on sitting in traffic. The Heathrow attacks were coordinated, as were New York and Saudi Arabia so it follows that they would have acted by now if they had a target lined up in London. Maximum impact?'

'So you are saying they ditched their vehicle somewhere due west and doubled back?' The MI5 head suggested.

'Precisely,' said Peters, savouring a tuna and cucumber sandwich. 'An obvious rouse to confuse us?'

'Yes. Too deliberate by far and they will know that we know that it is such a stunt.' Jim added after sipping his coffee. He would have liked a glass of Red but dared not ask. 'We must not forget that these people have coordinated the deadliest attacks since 9/11. They don't do random, everything has a purpose.'

Peters turned from the map to ask, 'how do I zero in on an area . . . where is the control function?' His mind was now in overdrive. The hovering Cobra aide advanced with a touch pad and gave a short demonstration. As he did so, the Prime Minister was alerted to his blinking desktop phone. Moments later, he left the room - 1600 Pennsylvania Avenue needed a discreet word.

'How does Heathrow connect with the attacks in New York and Saudi Arabia?' Jim asked the gathering.

'Not sure that is relevant to finding our terror cell Detective, just concentrate on what we have tasked you to do?' The Home Secretary gave a smug grin to the intel heads.

'If you want us to help, it would be smart to let us know the whole picture . . . sir.'

The Commissioner shot his subordinate a frosty look - a snowball smacking your face look.

'We don't want your help, we demand it.' The Home Secretary said mid-way through blowing his nose. 'And by the way, this committee did get along without you up to now . . . Mister Duke!'

'Yet my colleague and I are here, in the heart of government . . . Mister Fumbler.'

'Excuse me Brannigan?'

The room fell silent as Jenkins and Peters turned from the updating map.

'What did you just call the Home Secretary, Detective Brannigan?' The Commissioner enquired.

'He addressed me as "Duke" so I just presumed that not standing on ceremony, meant we are all okay with nicknames, sir?'

'You called me . . . "Fumbler", Detective?'

Jim's immediate boss gave him an imploring look this time, to no avail.

'Yes, Home Secretary. You are known to many of the Police Service as "The Fumbler" as a lot of us think you just fumble around in the dark . . . sir.'

There were a few discreet murmurs and an array of shocked faces around the table as they awaited the expected outburst. However, the Home Secretary chose his words carefully. 'One so called heroic act, your vigilante success in 1999, does not make you infallible . . . one good deed does not a hero make in my book Brannigan!'

'No problem, Home Secretary. I'll just keep an eye out on the media for your one good deed, shall I?'

As the Prime Minister returned, he witnessed the remnants of his Home Secretary's lengthy outburst at Jim's last aside. His presence brought the meeting to order but he did not waste time to ask what had occurred. Jenkins would bring him up to scratch following the meeting.

'That was the White House on the line gentlemen. Who the fuck is, or should I say was . . . Steve Ingram?'

Everyone took a breath during which a search was done on a government database. 'Ingram is . . . was? Ingram was one of our analysts sir,' the MI6 chief replied looking at his tablet. 'What happened to him?'

The PM opened a bottle of mineral water and used a palm-full to dampen his face. After taking a drink, he replied with pent up annoyance. 'I have to hear of the death of one of our people from the Americans?'

The Commissioner looked up from his personal tablet. 'He was clubbed and strangled by an intruder, a burglar so it seems?'

'What is the connection, Prime Minister?' Jenkins asked as he walked back to the conference table.

'The president's people believe he stumbled onto a connection to the attacks . . . that's bloody what!'

'I saw that report earlier today sir, it has all the trademarks of a cover-up.' Peters said as he continued his map perusal. 'Ingram's hard drive was removed but the main frame was left behind. A one-man job but I can't see our jihadists targeting an MI6 analyst as it would seem to indicate that they have someone inside Six? It doesn't wash with me gentlemen. It wasn't a burglar and it wasn't the terror cell. That said, I have no idea who it was. Maybe a domestic primed to look like an intruder? It's puzzling and I don't believe in coincidences like this.'

'Nor me,' remarked the PM. 'The Americans think he was on the trail of this assassin character . . . though what *he* has got to do with anything is beyond me.'

There was a collective sigh around the table.

'Assassin?' Jim enquired.

Jenkins received a nod of approval from the PM. 'A phantom hitman who has supposedly killed an unknown number of persons of note, detectives. I myself can't see such an individual, if he exists, toeing the Jihadist line. He would be an infidel to them.'

Peters turned from the display. 'Gentlemen, it seems confusion rules the day and that to my mind is . . .'

'Suspicious, with regard to what's happening at the moment.' Brannigan said reading his colleague's thoughts. 'And I am to take it that the CIA have people inside our own intelligence communities?'

'Oh please, what do you think Brannigan?' Scoffed the Home Secretary.

The MI6 controller looked at his MI5 counterpart who sat gazing over at Peters. 'Show me the agency that doesn't have a foreign mole, we all do it . . . it's the way the system works.'

'Have your two officers worked the same cases before?' Asked the tired looking Secretary of Defence.

'Not till today, sir,' replied Jim. 'I'm North West London and DCI Peters is Central. Our career paths have never crossed, case wise I mean. I know of him naturally and while he looks a peculiar looking article, he is a top notch copper.'

The PM gave a hint of a smirk, followed closely by the others, all except the Home Secretary.

As Peters, who had ignored the remark, returned to the multi-screen display, one of its screens flashed repeatedly. The Commissioner grabbed his phone receiver as the image of a Volvo saloon dominated the screen from the car wash area of the BP garage on the Heathrow ring road.

'It's a ruse . . . a warning of some effect?' Peters remarked calmly before he asked for an outside line. 'We are now looking for three separate individuals.'

'The cell has split up?' Brannigan asked his colleague. 'That is not good. We now have to trace three targets instead of one?'

'Explain please?'

Peters motioned for Brannigan to continue.

'Well Prime Minister, they had the transport to immediately make a dash for it, so to speak, using the back streets of Harlington and beyond, away from the motorways? They could have driven this Volvo to a different location while chaos ensued and then done whatever it was that was next on their agenda?' The PM nodded, though not really grasping the full meaning. Jim paused before adding, 'instead, they ditch the car at Heathrow?'

The committee waited for his reasoning. Peters wandered around the room, as was his way while placing himself inside the mind of a fugitive. He stopped suddenly and looked at Jim. 'There will be CCTV footage from that BP station which means they are showing themselves to us gentlemen. They want us to know what they look like.'

'Spot on Peters,' said Brannigan. 'And the reason they have done this is to have us chase them down while the real danger lies elsewhere.'

'Conjecture detectives,' the MI6 head remarked with the approval of a majority of the table.

'Don't dismiss it too quickly gents,' Jenkins said. 'What possible reason could they have for such a deliberate action?'

The aide arrived by his secret door and interrupted by pointing to the bank of screens. Several monitors showed CCTV images of three men exiting the Volvo while making sure to confront each and every camera on the petrol station's forecourt.

The MI6 spook bit his lip. 'Apologies officers! Continue with your thoughts?'

'Jim?' Peters said gazing at further recorded images of the three Arab looking men entering the BP shop to buy some goods, all the while facing a camera. 'Do you reckon they are still at Heathrow?'

Brannigan nodded.

'Fuck me! You mean they are hiding out there . . . after another target maybe?'

'Not necessarily Prime Minister.' Brannigan replied, 'they probably work . . . or live out there. There is a large Asian community out west, sir.'

The MI6 and MI5 men talked between themselves before the Vauxhall spook said. 'Good to have your thoughts officers . . . many hands make light work etcetera . . .'

'I'll qualify that remark. Nothing like good old fashioned detective work. What do you propose gents . . . not house-to-house I'm guessing?'

'Correct sir,' Peters answered, 'it would only spook them, forgive the pun.'

The intelligence director smiled before Brannigan took over.

'House to house, door to door would take too much time and most definitely alert the cell.' Jim said as hunger began to bite at him. 'We have to think of another tactic.'

The Prime Minister stood up. 'Okay, let's break for some food and brainstorm this . . . it's what we are here for. One obvious question before we do-'

'No sir, we cannot issue their images to the media. They are most likely seeking a hostage type scenario near the airport to divert attention from a deadlier threat, possibly in Central London.'

Everyone looked at Brannigan who had anticipated the Prime Minister's thoughts, some in surprise, others in annoyance, especially the Home Secretary.

'One last issue gentlemen,' the PM announced. 'As you have noticed, our Chief of Defence Staff is missing and will not be returning. A new appointment will be made when I met with Her Majesty.'

As the gathering left the conference room to eat, Jenkins and the PM sat together to discuss what occupied their minds once more. The unit - should the two officers be privy to Cobra's secret?

'I noticed that no one asked us privately about Assaf's wife and his bodyguards killings, Dave?'

'It is hardly a newsworthy item with all that's going on Bernard. What do you think of our esteemed Chief of the Defence Staff quitting?'

'He knew well that it was our TFB unit who took Assaf and murdered the wife and guard. He just didn't agree with it, never has done.'

'Old school military, Bernard. He was a good man but we'll get another shortly while his deputy fills in. One thing Britain is not short of is high ranking officers.'

## CHAPTER TEN

Muslim ritual demanded the burial of the deceased before the following sunset, usually within 24 hours of death. With this in mind, the Sheikh answered the call of his ruling cousin and now sat before him in the Royal Palace.

'We have to respect our faith and traditions Your Majesty but as the mall's victims body parts are still being identified beside the remains of non-Muslims I suggest we use extraordinary caution in dealing with the burials.'

The King looked around his extended family in the vast reception room, expecting to hear an objection from one of the many princes in attendance. As no one objected, he gave his approval. An extra detachment of palace guards stood to attention along the jewel adorned walls where priceless tapestries hung alongside royal family portraits.

'As you wish Your Majesty. It will appease the Westerners whose subjects died alongside our own.' The Sheikh felt a warm glow inside and pressed on. 'I take it that you will be attending one of the funerals?'

'Yes cousin, probably the twins who died outside the mall's jewellery outlet. Such sadness considering their mother survived the atrocity.'

'Very wise. It will probably be a security nightmare but while we hunt down these defilers of our sacred soil we will redouble our efforts to ensure our personal safety.'

The King of Saudi Arabia bade farewell to his cousin with the traditional Arab embrace. The Sheikh left the palace with his loyal entourage, knowing he would never see it in the same way again.

An hour later, in the air-conditioned safety of his official residence, the Sheikh sat in front of a brand new laptop. He was alone and had a message to read. From a dummy Facebook account set up with email alerts, he had obtained a copy of Oliver Twist, the English version, 'liked' earlier that day by his anonymous contract killer on the social network site. As he clicked on the infidel's chosen sleazy date site and keyed in his password, he saw the simple coded message from the assassin in the inbox. Using it, he configured the pages, lines, words and letters from Oliver Twist to decode the message.

*Further attacks unnecessary on my part. View as counterproductive. Repeat, further attacks unnecessary on my part.*

'Hmm,' replied the Saudi rebel as he methodically typed and corrected his reply.

*Understood, but not all my work. There are many besides myself who seek the downfall of the present status quo. The recent attacks have thrown the enemy into confusion. I fail to see how it does not assist you. Good hunting!*

The Sheikh smiled at his contrived message, congratulating himself on his English spelling. 'You will die too infidel when this is over,' he remarked as he shut down the laptop and clapped his hands.

An aide appeared and the pair walked slowly to the basement where the laptop was destroyed in their presence. One of hundreds of personal computers that he had obtained for his new world plan.

\*\*\*

Four thousand miles away in a quiet London suburb, the assassin decoded the Sheikh's response and simply rebooted his laptop before heading for the shower. As the warmth of the spray hit his lean and scarred body, he placed himself inside the mind of his Arab contractor. The Sheikh will probably try something and he would simply have to be two steps ahead, as was his nature. Capture and its consequences by clients, targets or the authorities was not an option. He towelled dry and placed an order for a vegetarian dish from a local restaurant. It was only a short distance away but he limited his comings and goings as a precaution. His two London safe houses had been meticulously sourced and bought, primarily because of the adjacent buildings - Metropolitan Police stations. Hiding in plain sight. North and South London addresses with identical kitchens and furnishings. Inside each dwelling was a false door built into the kitchen walls. Inside the small, covert cubbyholes were passports, currency, weapons and uniforms of different police units. In the event of his intruder alarm detecting an unwanted approach, he would release a smoke grenade before slipping into the false compartment. From there he would set off a minor explosion in the attic to emerge amid the chaos in the same dress code as his armed intruders. He doubted whether his elaborate plan would ever have to be enacted in either of his homes but safety was paramount. He had an Audi saloon permit-parked outside each house and identical Yamaha 750 motorcycles under canvas in his rear gardens. He knew the element of surprise lay with a possible intruder but he felt comfortable with the precautions he had in place. His tropical island retirement would demand nothing less.

After slowly digesting his meal, he lay back on his lounger to ponder his approach to the ninth target. Regardless of whatever treachery the Sheikh probably had in mind, he would continue with his planning, as he was honour bound to do so. As he relaxed to the faint hush of Barbara Streisand, he dwelled on the Arab's intentions. His deception would not be to avoid paying the remaining twenty five million as it was small change to him - it was the fact that he would have a loose end out there. An infidel to boot! He would carry on with his task, secretly hoping that the Sheikh had some degree of latitude in avoiding further unnecessary attacks. Collateral damage was always a concern but what he had perpetrated in London, New York and his Saudi homeland was just bloodlust to whip up his loyal followers. For the first time in years, he had regrets about taking a job, despite the incredible paradise retirement sum involved. It is not as if he enjoyed killing, except the most monstrous of targets, it was a job, like any other. A job that was dangerous but extremely rewarding. But was this worth it? He began to get that itchy feel beneath his scalp when his mobile phone bleeped. The intel conversation lasted all but two minutes. He was content with the information and pulled down an A to Z of London from his bookrack to check out his route. Something is wrong, he proposed to himself as he gathered his equipment and prepared to leave.

\*\*\*

The favourite in the third greyhound race at Walthamstow slumped to the dirt as the electronic circuit released the six traps. The dog, Simchuk's pride and joy, had been dosed earlier in the kennels by Sara Brahms as the meeting was about to begin. As predicted, the Albanian mobster arose from his comfortable position in a balcony VIP box and went outside to gain a better view of the furore that was taking place thirty feet below. As the gang lord stepped out, Steve Cooper placed his finger on the trigger of his McMillan TAC .338 sniping weapon and steadied his aim. The 'Mac' as he referred to it, discharged lethal Lapua Magnum rounds, guaranteed to destroy his target, just over half a mile away.

'Let's see what we got under the hood tonight, shall we Miss Brahms?'

Sara, crouched beside him in an unoccupied tower block, spoke into her collar com. Just as she received the order to execute, she heard a cracking sound instantly followed by a thud and then felt her face awash with the odour and slickness of Steve's blood. All she heard, other than the corner window's small crack and thud was the whoosh of the bullet that took apart her colleague's head. Steve 'Coop' Cooper had met his end, courtesy of a sniper from a similar council tower block far off to their left. The unknown rifleman had been waiting. Brahms hit the floor and crawled towards the graffiti sprayed far wall. She took one look behind her, knowing Cooper was beyond help and spoke into her com.

'Be advised, man down, man down! Seek immediate evac. Out!'

**'Roger that, en route to you now.'**

Within ten minutes, Sara and Steve's remains had been removed by the remaining unit members. Only Zorin was missing, having remained at base.

'How the fuck did Simchuk know we had him in our sights?' Keegan asked, looking down at Cooper's body bag in the back of their adapted Range Rover.

'What's more,' Harris snarled, 'are we compromised? Does Simchuk or whoever is responsible for this attack know of our base?'

Sara, still shaken and using wipes to clean her face and neck shook her head. 'I can't see that we would be compromised as whoever killed Coop would have targeted us all at the house before this.'

'I see your logic Sara but can we take the risk to return there now?' Keegan asked as he thought back on his personal memories of his American friend.

'Yakov would have sent us a distress signal by now if Stanley Hall had even been recce'd . . . surely?' Cooney said as he steered the high-powered motor towards the North Circular Road. 'What's it to be boss?'

'Head west Seamus. Sara, contact Yakov on the landline, code-in.'

After just two rings, the Russian picked up the phone.

'Is that Stanley's Cab office?' Sarah asked with a tinge of anxiety.

The safe immediate response of "sorry, you have the wrong number again" meant there was no coercion, no imminent threat.

**'Sorry, you have the wrong number again.'** The Russian replied and hung up.

After the line went dead, Sara's mobile rang. It was Zorin's mobile, following protocol. **'All is fine here. Why the code-in Sara?'**

'Trouble friend . . . big trouble. Our ETA approximately thirty to forty. Stay alert Yakov.' Harris said after taking the phone.

'Boss!' The Russian answered before ending the call.

\*\*\*

As Jenkins sat with the PM over their beef casserole, his mobile buzzed. He answered it and listened to Kenneth Harris, his face haunted, his shoulders slumped.

'What's wrong?' The PM asked after he ended the call.

The dapper civil servant explained what had happened to a unit member at Walthamstow and pushed aside his plate.

'What the fuck were they doing at a dog track?' The Prime Minister whispered menacingly. 'I thought they were interrogating the Assaf fucker?'

'One of them was sir, while the others finished off the Albanian affair. They always complete their tasks, as you know, no loose ends. Assaf has a weak heart and he is no use to us dead. He spoke of a Sheikh, identity unknown but if he knows something, the unit will get it from him. They have to tread lightly.'

Both men looked around the impromptu dining room at the other committee members seated at similar tables. Would they have to be told?

'Who was killed Bernard, which one?'

'I thought we never did specifics, sir?'

'Just curious . . . he worked for us, albeit covertly-'

'Denial, Prime Minister . . . always remember - denial. It was the American.'

'The SEAL sniper was shot by a *sniper* . . . shit! That's fucked up!'

'Something does not add up, sir. Kenneth Harris and I doubt that the Albanians could arrange that . . . or even find them in the first place-'

'Are you suggesting the unit has been compromised, Bernard?'

'Eh . . . no, of course not, Dave. That would be impossible, as the only people who know of their existence are all Cobra committee. And the unit do not discuss the unit with anyone themselves-'

'What makes you so sure, Bernard?'

'Themselves. Don't forget Dave, I've met them and believe me they are mute and besides, they have nobody to tell.'

'And Sir Raymond Blanch, would he have told anyone about them?'

'You jest Dave, he would be ruined if it came out that he sponsored a vigilante unit that we used intermittently.'

'You are right. We'll just have to presume that the Albanian thug was more capable than the unit thought he was.'

'For the moment, sir.'

'Now Bernard, this tricky situation regarding the detectives' knowledge of the unit?'

'Yes, Prime Minister?' Jenkins replied tentatively.

'We're kidding ourselves if we think we can withhold all relevant information from everybody working on this affair. The threat is so great which means that everyone has to be in the loop. Brannigan and Peters are bound by the official secrets act and will have to be made aware of the unit's existence.'

'So who is going to have the unenviable task of telling two PC plods that Her Majesty's government use contract killers to do our dirty work?'

The PM's blank expression gave away the answer. He walked from the suite and plunged himself behind his office desk. He looked down at the phone, wondering - *will I get the call or should I do it myself.* The Monarch had little say in government but pressure could still be applied. He relaxed in his chair thinking of Churchill's defiance and Thatcher's resolve. *Why on my shift?* It seemed that fate had laid a trap, a suffocating hold on him that he knew he would not survive. Right at that moment, he instinctively knew that he would use any and all means to end the mayhem. You treat fire with fire, but a SEAL sniper shot dead by another sniper? Who could do that . . . who was capable of such an act? The Prime Minister of Great Britain picked up his phone and placed a transatlantic call. Ten frustrating minutes later, he hung up and called for his personal secretary.

'Get the Palace on the line,' he said. 'Get me an appointment, right away.'

'Yes sir, may I ask why?'

'No.' He answered, knowing that if all his resources and even the denial unit could not deal with the situation, then he had no option. He sensed that the body count would only get worse and for the first time in his adulthood, he truly wished he had never entered the political arena. An unseen enemy was the worst kind and right at that precise moment he had no idea of how to avoid more chaos. How would Bush and Blair have been remembered if 9/11 had never happened? How would their terms have progressed? The world had changed and things were only going to get worse. His thoughts swayed from decision to indecision as he steadied himself to leave his office for the short trip down the Mall. This was not how it was supposed to have been.

## CHAPTER ELEVEN

After the Queen had refused to accept her Prime Minister's resignation, he steadied himself, accepting the reality that he would serve out his term. No one in government knew of his offer and his increasing weariness in dealing with an unseen enemy. The Cobra conference suite fell silent as Bernard Jenkins finished his debriefing for the benefit of the two London detectives. Peters had sat bemused through the speech but Jim Brannigan had privately simmered.

'Is this the fucking twilight zone or what? Have you all gone loopers?'

'Excuse me Detective?' The Deputy Prime Minister asked, 'what did you just say?'

Jim let go of a deep breath, recalling his 1999 clash with the former SAS unit who had captured the public's imagination by killing gangsters, terrorists and child abusers. The elite trio had been mentored by high-ranking former police and army kingpins. He pushed back his chair and got to his feet.

I asked if you bunch of James Bond fuckwits were living in the twilight zone?'

How dare you!' His police commissioner responded standing up to face him. You will work with us Brannigan or I will have your pension.'

Take it!'

'Never mind your pension, your family won't have a roof over their heads tonight if you cross us, detective,' the MI6 director added. 'And we can hold you for obstructing the course of justice.'

Brannigan walked over to the spook and spun his chair around. 'Just think of that word you just used . . . justice?'

The spy was about to stand up when the Prime Minister intervened.

'Detective, please retake your seat. Listen to what I have to say before you make any rash decisions.'

'What's to stop me going to the media and revealing this whole sordid affair? Why should I stay here, I have broken no laws?'

'Because I am the Prime Minister and I am asking you to hear me out. That's why and whether you like me or even voted for me . . . I am still head of the government.'

'Please Jim,' Peters said with a grimace, 'listen to what he has to say?'

'I can't believe what I have heard here tonight!' Jim scowled as he sat back into his chair. '*Task Force Black!* Which of you Walter Mitty types thought up that beauty?'

'You have an ego problem Brannigan!' The Home Secretary said, 'I don't agree with this murderous unit but I follow orders . . . for the common good.'

The PM cleared his throat and glared at Jenkins who seemed genuinely shocked. He had thought his speech was rather eloquent and would appeal to the officer's sense of national pride.

'Do you agree in principle that we have to use every effort, every means at our disposal to catch the terrorists and prevent further carnage?'

'Every legitimate force, yes! But not these thugs . . . a former IRA bomber and a Russian deserter who interrogates people,' Jim was getting angrier by the second. 'Hold on a second . . . does the Queen and her family know about this shit?'

'No, only Cobra members know and only myself and the Prime Minister know of the unit's location. When I am no longer here, my successor will find those details in my safe.' Bernard Jenkins said in a lethargic tone.

'Let me get this straight in my head?' Brannigan said as he reached for his cold coffee. 'Let me give my summation of what is going on here, yeah?'

The PM nodded, the others remained silent. All eyes were on Brannigan.

'Haroon Rashid Assaf who planned the 7/7 London bombings is being interrogated right now by a gang of . . . let me see, an ex SEAL, a former Mossad agent, *a former IRA bomber* . . . stop me if I miss anyone out?'

Jenkins gave a wry smile and the PM nodded to Jim to continue.

'A Spetsnaz torturer and two former British Special Forces backed by a crazy rich anonymous benefactor? Right so far?'

'Cooper, the SEAL sniper was shot and killed last night,' Jenkins said.

'Who shot him . . . do the Heathrow terror cell know of the existence of this Cobra Task . . . Force Black?' Peters asked as he arose and walked to the electronic monitor bank.

'We don't know who shot him Peters, the unit was targeting an Albanian mob at the time.' Jenkins replied.

'So this unit murders people in the UK which the government can then disavow. Gangsters . . . who else?' Peters asked with his back to the table.

Jenkins ignored the remark and looked intently at Brannigan. 'I know your feelings on vigilantism Jim but can you not see that we have to fight fire with fire? These jihadists-'

'Not a chance! Never! May I be excused, Prime Minister?'

'Detective Brannigan, take a look at the whole jigsaw before throwing out a piece.'

The cop sighed. 'Edmund Burke once said, "Justice is itself the one great standing of civilized policy and any eminent departure from it, under any circumstances, lies under the suspicion of being no policy at all."'

The PM stood up and beckoned Jim over to the door of the suite. 'Come with me please, Detective Brannigan?'

While the committee brainstormed the cell's next possible move, a call arrived from an official at Cheltenham's GCHQ global surveillance station. A telephone conversation had been intercepted between two individuals relating to the Heathrow bombings.

The Prime Minister ushered DCI Jim Brannigan into his private office at ten Downing Street. 'I have something I would like you to see, Brannigan.' He opened a secure cabinet and carried from it an armful of green folders; each tied with red ribbon and marked ***Cobra Chair - Eyes Only*** in the centre. He poured himself a neat Scotch after placing the folders on his desk next to Jim. 'You are a red wine man I hear?'

Hmm?' Jim looked up from the first of the folders that he had opened.

Would you like a glass of Red, Jim?'

Why not, it seems a nice way to bow out.'

The PM's desk phone rang. 'Yes, Bernard?' As he held the phone to his ear, the PM poured a generous amount of a Saint-Émilion into an adequate glass. 'Right, give me ten minutes and I'll be back with you.'

'Thanks,' Jim said accepting the wine. His eyes were glued to a case file he recognised from 2012. He read the details of a man who had killed two Russian dissidents in London of that year. He had poisoned them and had planned to kill a further ten dissidents with a bomb in a Piccadilly pub the next day. Despite intensive investigations, official sources had failed to capture the former Russian 'diplomat' until a woman called Sara Brahms led the 'unit' to the pub in the heart of the capital and another member had defused the bomb. There had been over 100 late night revellers in the bar at the time. Jim paused to taste his wine. 'Wow, that's better than what I am used to.'

'The wife's I'm afraid, I can't claim credit, not a wine man.'

'I'll take a case of this stuff instead of my pension-'

'Nobody is taking your pension detective, I will see to that. It is your right to voice your opinion. That's what we do here, preserve democracy.'

'Was using this rogue unit preserving democracy?' Jim asked holding up the folder, evidence of the unit's work.

'The preservation of up to one hundred lives I would say. We had failed to find the killer but they did, that's a fact.'

'What happened to the Russian lunatic? I never saw anything else on the news about this except the death of the two poisoned dissidents.'

'He "disappeared" . . . as the spooks would say.'

'You mean your contract unit murdered him?'

'I have access to these case folders but I never involve myself. Bernard Jenkins is the link man and he does not fill me in on everything.'

'I can't be dissuaded from my opinion on these matters, Prime Minister. I believe in law and order. There is no other way . . . otherwise anarchy will eventually prevail.'

'If the unit had not caught that Russian, a lot of lives would have been lost Jim.'

'Yes sir, I can see that. I mean, if they only did surveillance work I would understand but "disappearing" people on British soil is . . .?'

'Speaking of Bernard by the way, that call was from him. GCHQ intercepted a Heathrow related call-'

'Between?' Jim asked impulsively after savouring a mouthful of the grape.

'Saudi Arabia and-'

'West London?'

'Yes. You and Peters were correct, would you believe, Feltham.'

'That's barely a mile from Heathrow!'

\*\*\*

Ten minutes passed before the Prime Minister strode back into the conference suite, followed by Jim Brannigan, clutching a suspiciously large mug. An agreement had been reached.

'Gentlemen,' the PM announced. 'DCI Brannigan is going to continue working on detecting the terror cell and is then going to take early retirement from the Police Force on completion of his duty, with all his privileges. He has my assurance on this and I have his that his difference of opinion on the morality of this venture is noted for my successors in this office. Now, what news of Feltham?'

As the Police Commissioner was about to speak, the PM added, 'and may I also thank DCI Peters for his diligence in this stressful situation we find ourselves in.'

Peters returned from the bank of plasma screens to see Jim sitting back in his chair cradling his mug. 'A drop of red and you are anybody's Brannigan!'

'I was thinking of packing it in at some stage Maurice. I don't agree with this rogue unit malarkey but as the Prime Minister pointed out, lives are at stake. I won't be there for the kill, I've seen enough death to last me.'

'Nor will I Jim, we are merely investigating after all.'

'When you two have finished applauding yourselves, maybe we can get back to work?' The Commissioner said with a trace of annoyance in his voice. The PM was the boss but they were his officers.

'GCHQ could not give us an exact location in Feltham Prime Minister and the Saudi locale was Riyadh but it is a start.'

'What were the exact words, Bernard?'

He pointed to a screen's transcript -

*"diver--on   for   --am-d   i-----l   warran---.   Ex---te   m----r di---s-on.   Heathr-- ac-ion   pra--ed."*

'That's it?'

'Yes, Prime Minister,' the MI6 head answered, 'it was garbled but we do know that it was a Yemini Arabic accent as opposed to just plain Arabic.'

'Can we see the original English script?' Peters asked.

'It was in English, Detective.'

'Strange-'

'Not only strange Peters, and nor was it accidental. It was purposely done and the word "Heathrow" mentioned deliberately.' Jim observed. 'As if they knew it would set alarm bells ringing in Cheltenham?'

Peters' mind was ablaze with connotations. 'They are toying with us. When you say the conversation was garbled . . . do you mean a bad connection?'

The MI6 chief consulted his notes. 'No, there were background noises that truncated certain syllables of the indistinguishable words. GCHQ picked up everything that they could pick up.'

'Is there any hope of listening to the audio tape?' Jim asked.

Jenkins gave a nod and the MI6 man's tablet blurted out the recording, which they left on repeated play.

The MI5 representative used his remote and pointed to another screen. 'The call only lasted a few seconds, which is suspicious in itself. Both were cell phones, which are now dead. It's fresh intel but this is what our agencies have come up with as of one minute ago.'

*"diversion for diamond i-----l warranted. Execute m----r diversion. Heathrow action praised."*

'What do you make of the missing words, Alex?' The PM asked his recently appointed head of MI6.

'We are working on it sir, shouldn't be that difficult. Probably ten to fifteen minutes-'

'Infidel and minor.'

All heads looked up to see Peters who remained standing in front of the screens. The Commissioner smiled.

'Yes . . . yes, well done that man!' The Deputy PM said as he tore up his own calculations. 'But what does "diamond infidel" actually mean?'

'It means that your mythical assassin . . . killer or whatever might be factual.'

'How so Jim?' Jenkins asked.

'The Yanks said that Ingram was killed and it might be connected to Heathrow, correct?'

No one spoke so Jim continued as Peters came back to the table. 'It is known that contract killers were sometimes paid in diamonds or gold rather than currencies to avoid a money trail . . . so maybe this phantom killer is actually working for this mysterious Sheikh character that your thugs got out of Assaf?'

'Mmn, interesting Brannigan,' responded the MI5 man. 'It's tenuous but I am not a fan of coincidences either, just like your colleague, DCI Peters.'

Peters spoke next. 'Would it be possible for Brannigan and I to interrogate this Assaf chap ourselves?'

'Totally out of the question,' Bernard Jenkins replied sharply. 'Part of the disavow clause means we never . . . ever interfere in their operations.'

'You just get them to do your dirty work,' Brannigan said, receiving a hapless look from the PM.

'That's a shame,' said Peters. 'I would love to have a crack at him. I remember the rumours of an Arab UK resident being the instigator of the attacks but they died down quickly. Do you all believe that Assaf was involved in the 7/7 London bombings?'

The general murmur of approval provoked the DCI to enquire. 'Why wasn't he charged?'

'Lack of evidence, to put it bluntly. One of the papers did an expose on him . . . it was The Mail or Telegraph I think.' The Deputy PM remarked looking at his watch.

'Okay, back to Feltham gentlemen. How do we go about locating and flushing this cell out without more loss of life?'

'We wait for GCHQ, Prime Minister. To see if they can narrow our scope.'

'I agree with Peters,' Jenkins mused. 'I presume you have spotters on the way?'

The MI5 chief and his MI6 counterpart reacted with brief, sketchy details of agents posing as cab drivers, street sweepers, ordinary pedestrians, charity collectors, data researchers, coffee shop watchers and a small scattering of homeless street dwellers who would be in place within the hour. Feltham had a population of approximately 28,000 so it would be a gradual influx of agents - anywhere up to 200 operatives by the day's end. Eyes and ears on the ground were as effective as satellites sweeping the surface of the earth or digital face recognition.

## CHAPTER TWELVE

Seamus Cooney drove past the main gate of Stanley Hall and pulled over beneath the shadow of a large roadside oak tree.

'Do your thing Sara,' Harris ordered, motioning for Keegan to accompany her.

The former Mossad agent walked over to the gate and used her iPhone to film the sparsely lit mansion and the driveway that led up to the entrance. Once completed she got back in the Range Rover and compared the thirty-second footage with the previous thirty-second footage taken the night before that she had sent to all her colleagues' phones. She held Harris' aloft and pressed play on both devices, looking for any anomalies. It was their tedious task to complete whenever the majority of the unit were away from their base for an extended period. An extra set of tyre marks, a broken shrub or a curtain's setting would be enough to justify alarm. Yakov or whoever remained alone at the site would stay inside and never touch a curtain or change any of the appearance of the building's view from the road. If there had been any intrusion, the intruders might haplessly leave a difference.

'We're good to go boss.' Sara said activating the main gate after checking simultaneous clips of footage.

'Yakov, we're coming in!'

**'Copy that sir!'** The Russian replied and released the door's locking system.

'Where will we bury him?' Yakov asked later as he zipped up Cooper's body bag. It was the only time the others had seen genuine sadness on the face of the former Spetsnaz veteran.

'Can I tell you all something quite unbelievable?' Kenneth Harris said as they walked back from the caterer sized refrigerator unit where they had placed their comrade.

Yakov, Cooney, Brahms and Keegan sat on or leant against high stools in the vast kitchen waiting for his revelation. Before he did so, he broke one of their rigid rules by handing each a glass of Southern Comfort with ice, Cooper's favourite tipple.

During all the planning that went into this unit's setup and through every subsequent operation, never once did I plan for this day when one of us would need a decent burial. Not once did I think of it . . . never crossed my mind.'

The four of them knew he felt responsible though they were all still clueless as to how they had been spotted.

'Here's to Coop!' Harris raised his glass.

To Coop!'

They drank and paused for a short silence.

'Sara, Yakov . . . with me.' Harris said with a distinct menace.

The three of them descended to the basement where Haroon Rashid Assaf lay sleeping.

'I wouldn't want to be that fucker down there tonight,' said Cooney as he helped Keegan prepare a meal that they presumed would be barely touched due to a distinct lack of appetite.

'Do you think the Albanians had a hand in Coops death, Irish?'

'Not a chance David. From what Sara said it was a clean shot to the head from an angle of at least three to four hundred yards.'

'My thought exactly Seamus. But who the fuck is capable of that and how did they know we were there?'

'I know mate . . . who uses an 8.58 round bolt action from that distance?'

'That was a contract kill Irish. Someone has eyes on us.'

\*\*\*

A young beat constable greeted the familiar face as he entered the house opposite his Kentish Town police station.

Once inside the house, the assassin placed his McMillan TAC .338 rifle inside his kitchen's false compartment and placed a call to an all-night takeaway in Camden Town. He showered quickly and got to the door just as the delivery driver pressed his bell. As he ate his shrimp and noodle dish, he reflected on the evening's events. When he had reached the dog track, he had walked around for a while trying to figure how the Albanian would be assassinated and it did not take long to figure out a high rise shot. From the car park, he used his scope to scan the perimeter and then the high-rise estates in the distance. Eventually, he saw a man and a woman enter a disused council home on the eight floor of a tenement block. Without the scope, he would never have noticed their movement. He had thought of entering the flat to surprise them with his Browning pistol but he was unsure of their backup, if any. Hence, he decided on a headshot. It was an irony that when he reached his vantage point and looked through his scope he saw the American with the exact same rife. He had hoped to cut down the woman as she fled the flat but she had played it cool and waited for back up so he withdrew. He had been given all relevant details of the Albanian and he would have preferred to have targeted him instead but a job was a job.

As the Sheikh's contract killer prepared to rest for the night, he thought of the man's life he had taken and wondered if they had ever met. He had known a SEAL Team Six warrant officer who possessed a photographic memory and as he put his head on his pillow, he wished he had such a gift. Instead, he practised what he termed 'memory recall' where he focussed on an image and placed himself in past locations where he could possibly have seen a certain type of individual.

A further irony was that as the killer swept his memory for a link, DCI Jim Brannigan returned to Kentish Town police station in the dead of night to collect a few personals before heading for a quick nap to the house where his wife Teresa and son John lay slumbering and clueless as to his participation in the largest manhunt in British criminal history. He could not tell Teresa a word of what was going on, even though she knew his disrupted routine meant something was afoot. He would tell her that he was taking early retirement and finally accepting the comfortable salaried job as a security consultant for a city banking house. If his government was using vigilantes, he was powerless to stop them, but he would not remain part of the establishment knowing what he now knew. However, principles aside, the terror cell had to be located and he would fulfil his promise to the Prime Minister.

\*\*\*

'What's so hush-hush that you can't tell your own wife about?' Teresa asked Jim over his dreaded muesli breakfast. He had slept for four hours and woke up tired with the same darkness seeping through their lounge window.

'I can't say love, it's that simple. I could tell you a lie but you know that's not my style.'

'Okay,' she replied pouring two filtered coffees, 'just tell me that it's not dangerous. Can you do that?'

I can say that I am not in any danger so let's leave it at that. I am going to have to get going shortly love.'

Do you really believe that you will be content working a city security job . . . after all these years nicking people? Don't kid yourself sweetheart.'

I've had it Teresa, things have changed. The world is different now and by the way, I'll be gone all day again.'

Mrs Brannigan straightened her husband's tie, 'I will be content with the extra money and you will have more time at home but I just can't picture you as anything other than a copper.'

Get used to it-'

Hold on a second Mister . . . what about the Mansion House lunch?'

Fuck it, I forgot about that. That's still two days away. . . I might be free by then. I just don't know right now.'

Well you had better be because I am not letting my mum down and sis is looking forward to seeing John.'

You okay to take him to school?'

'Yes, why wouldn't I?'

Brannigan drove towards Whitehall and the Cobra suite pondering his wife's words. He knew he would regret walking away while the terror cell was still at large and he had concerns about his wife and son even attending a public function while the alert status level remained at critical. His thoughts came back to him as BBC radio 5Live announced breaking news from Saudi Arabia.

*"News is coming in of a series of explosions in Riyadh. The reports have yet to be confirmed but the target seems to have been the funeral of one of the victims . . ."*

Jim turned on his siren and floored the accelerator.

'Is it true?' He asked the Home Secretary as he walked through to the Cobra conference suite. 'The radio said that the Saudi king was believed to be among the funeral victims.'

'I think it is Jim,' the minister replied using his first name for the first time. 'This is going to create a shit storm.'

The mood was sombre as the room sat and watched one of the plasma screen's Sky reports of the latest Saudi terror attack. Jim ambled across to a sleepy looking Peters who was pouring both a coffee.

'Any more insight into Feltham, Maurice?' Jim whispered discreetly.

'We are being played Jim, as you know.'

'This Sheikh character?'

'Who knows mate, but I do know one thing, you and I should be out there doing our job, not stuck in here playing mind games. We are a step behind these jihadists all day long.'

'I know, but it's the way these people play it, sitting in here watching their screens. You and I could get more from Assaf than the torturer could. If he's a true believer, then he will welcome martyrdom rather than give up this scary Sheikh.'

'You say it as if you already believe he exists and is behind this thing, Jim.'

'Well when you add a sudden wave of terrorism to the supposed veneration of this Sheikh by Assaf, it makes sense.'

'Gentlemen,' announced the PM, 'the Foreign Secretary will be joining us this morning for an update from Riyadh. I can confirm however, that Saudi Arabia has lost their king and thirty members of his immediate family. It was an airborne assault by suicidal fanatics who dropped their ordinance onto the funeral and then circled back to crash the site. As you can see from the crater on the news broadcasts, it caused utter devastation. Ah, here is the man for this task.'

An aide showed the Foreign Secretary to his seat where he immediately began his debrief. The pin stripped suit he had been due to wear to Washington hung loosely to his slumped frame. Everyone was feeling the effects of recent days, yearning for past years where a prison riot or a flood had been their most pressing concern.

'Good morning. As some of you may know, the Saudi thrown came with the title of "Custodian of The Two Holy Mosques" which to put it bluntly leaves us perilously close to war in the Middle East. Fingers are being pointed at Israel and Al Qaeda naturally but Saudi sources are also looking at Iran and ISIS amongst others. There is even talk of a secular revolution.'

'An inside job?' The PM enquired.

'Possibly sir, not sure as of now. Our embassy and Washington have offered the assistance of FBI and Special Branch but we have heard nothing back as of ten minutes ago. It's a . . . I can't quite think of an adequate word, gentlemen, even though I searched my brain on the way over here. It's the nearest we've been to 9/11 in fourteen years. The Home Secretary and Commissioner have something to say so I will yield to them. Thank you.'

The Commissioner closed his file and placed it on the desk. 'I think my remit will be better covered by my colleague.'

The Home Secretary used the remote to amplify the bank of screens into one. 'Considering this latest news, we have to expect another strike on our soil. With that in mind, I sadly propose that we leave our airspace closed for another twenty-four hours at the minimum and place army units at the terminals. We have no alternative other than to keep in place restricted public transport with city-wide check points on the roads. It's going to cause further bedlam but our alert level has to remain at critical. The Americans basically locked down Washington during the night. We are in deep this time.'

All heads turned to their leader.

'I spoke to the Chancellor before we came in. The effect this lockdown is going to have on our economy is going to be horrendous but public safety comes first. I am ordering extra Special Branch and a troop of 22 SAS to Feltham on standby. We have to have closure on these fuckers. Has anybody come up with anything new . . . and I mean new on how to flush this terror cell out?'

The table occupants began to talk amongst themselves leaving the Foreign Secretary the chance to approach DCI Brannigan.

'Good morning detective.'

'Good morning Minister,' Jim said putting his cup down and accepting the hand of the Foreign Secretary.

'I am honoured to meet you again.'

'Again, sir?'

'Yes, 1999 . . . after the vigilante business. I was at the debrief and we spoke?'

'Apologies sir, that was a shaky time. But, I am aware that you know my wife.'

'Yes indeed. A fantastic lady if I might add. I am a huge fan of Teresa Brannigan. She has raised more money for the present Ebola fund than all of those city bigwigs together.'

'Charity is her thing sir . . . since she left the police service herself. I think she would have gone out of her mind with boredom,' Jim didn't know exactly what to say when talking about his wife to other people so he simply added, 'thank you for your kind words Minster, I will pass them along.'

'I will relay them myself tomorrow night at the Mansion House. You will be there yourself?'

'I'm . . . I'm not entirely sure sir.' Jim's mind spun. 'Are you continuing with public events with this lockdown in place?'

'It will be maximum security Jim. There will be more police and security officials there than fundraisers I'm afraid to say but we can't curtail our democratic privileges entirely due to three lunatics-'

'Is the Prime Minister attending, sir?'

The Foreign Secretary looked across at his beleaguered party boss and leader of the government and shook his head. 'I doubt it but have no fears for Teresa. It would be a brave jihadist to take on that woman. A decorated former police officer who took you on, for better or worse!'

Jim could not help but smile at the remark but still felt uneasy about his wife attending a charity fundraiser in the city.

***

The assassin was awoken from his slumber by the single number on his Sheikh contact mobile. He answered it and memorised the latest intel.

Skipping breakfast except for an extra sweet cappuccino from a quick and easy packet, he set about readying the instrument of death he would use that day. The sniper was dead and his next target had been selected. He flicked the television remote and instinctively knew who was behind the horror that echoed from his screen. The BBC's Middle Eastern correspondent was talking over a scene of indescribable destruction. Over three hundred people had died and twice as many injured in the attacks from the sky. He had not seen a crater that big since his last foray into Iraq.

The fucking madman! He'll kill us all.'

He paused from his meticulous preparation, meditating on the enormity of what he had become involved in. Anyone willing to take out a head of state, a king . . . at a funeral. He had no great affection for the Saud family as he viewed them and the Iranians as the worst case sponsors of terrorism since the fall of the Soviet Union.

'Fucking lunatic!'

His instinct told him to carry on but be extra, extra vigilant. The Sheikh obviously had ears, a traitor at the heart of the UK government, who was supplying intelligence - he was a fanatic, a fanatic with untold wealth. A dangerous man.

# CHAPTER THIRTEEN

Despite being 'water boarded' during the night, Haroon Rashid Assaf had remained silent. They had not once referred to the London 7/7 bombings; all the questions had been about the Sheikh.

'Here is your last meal, shithead.' Yakov Zorin said tossing an uncooked pork chop through the tightly knit bars of his cell. 'See how hungry you are.'

'Fuck you, Russian pig!' Assaf replied throwing the meat at his bars. 'You soldier boys are worried? The Sheikh is coming . . . isn't he?'

I would have eaten that if I were you because the next meal around here is going to be *you*. My cats are hungry and that pork would have added flavour . . . get your virgin speech ready, shithead!'

'Pig!'

'See you at dinner, Arab!'

The giant Spetsnaz man flicked off the base light and headed for the ground floor monitors. The rest of the team had split up and gone their separate ways. Harris and Sara had received notice from Jenkins to check in to a Twickenham guesthouse in readiness for a possible recce of the Feltham area. Cooney and Keegan were heavily armed and headed for an Albanian run casino in East

London where they would either find Simchuk or one of his cohorts and extract any information regarding Cooper's death.

\*\*\*

The digital clock above the Cobra wall bank of screens relayed the time of various capitals around the world. It was 7:18 in Riyadh and 4:18 in London. The news from the Saudi capital via the Foreign Office was that the deputy crown prince of the house of Saud had taken control and had declared a curfew. The succession of the next in line to the throne was a complicated affair as the crown prince himself was in a coma. The religious police roamed the streets of the cities, shooting at anything that moved or shone a light. Desperation was in the air as there were increasing rumours of a distant cousin making a bid for the throne.

Jim's mobile beeped and he looked around to see who had noticed before looking at the caller display. 'Do you mind, Prime Minister, it is the wife?'

'Not at all detective, use next door for privacy.'

'Hi honey, what's up?'

**'Hey! Nothing much, except your son wants to wear a tuxedo to tomorrow night's event-'**

'Where are you?'

'Oxford Street, shopping in Selfridges for tomorrow night. He's not getting a tux, but I am getting those shoes . . . the ones we saw in the Sandra Bullock film?'

'Film? What are you doing Teresa . . . we're not even sure tomorrow's night fundraiser is going ahead yet.'

'Who is we, Bigtime?'

'Em, the government. We are still at a critical alert level, love. Why don't you put off shopping until the all clear is given?'

'Where are you now, darling?'

Jim never lied to his wife but had to do so now. 'Scotland Yard, at a security conference.'

'Can you join us for a quick bite to eat, darling?'

Jim's eardrum was assaulted by a loud bang. 'Teresa? Teresa . . . what was that?'

He was speaking to a dead line. He showed his ID badge to the security in the hall and went outside to see if the mobile reception was any better. After trying a few times, he went back to the room adjacent to the Cobra suite.

He redialled Teresa's number for a tenth time, growing more anxious every time he heard an automated **"the line is busy, please try later"** message.

The door suddenly opened and Maurice Peters shot his head around the door.

'Jim . . . you have to see this!'

'Hold on a minute Peters, I'm trying to call the wife back.'

'Now Brannigan, we've just been attacked again.'

'What . . . where?'

'Central London, Oxford Street and also Kensington . . .'

Jim sped past him in haste. He arrived in the conference suite to see a SKY news anchor speaking with a yellow banner displaying breaking news across the bottom.

\*\*\*

David Keegan nursed his bruised knuckles as he steered the Range Rover through to the North Circular Road turn off. He and Seamus Cooney were as shocked as they could possibly be, listening to the radio's updating reports of another terrorist attack on British soil. They had raided the Albanian casino and after knocking about a few of Simchuk's thugs, they had set about their leader, a trusted lieutenant of the mobster. Keegan had broken everything but his spine in an effort to trace Simchuk but it was the same old story. The Albanian didn't know where his boss was and if he did - he would not tell.

Cooney had been struck by a snooker ball while dealing with a hidden thug but it had no effect as he listened to the broadcast. 'Fuck me English . . . this is going to escalate.'

Fucking right it will Seamus. London again, after that Saudi massacre this morning. It's shit like this that could lead us back to war.'

The Irishman's mobile rang. It was Harris, again.

**Get back to base lads and remember to code-in on the landline with Yakov. Don't rush it because of what's going on. Sara and I will keep you updated on what we are going to do. This is a fucking nightmare.'**

Copy that boss!'

It took over an hour for their Range Rover to reach the tree line opposite Stanley Hall. Keegan rang the house's landline.

After five rings, the Russian answered the phone.

Is that Stanley's Cab office?' The former SAS man asked in a sarcastic tone.

**Sorry, you have the wrong number again.'** Yakov replied and hung up.

After the line went dead, Keegan's mobile rang out. It was Zorin's mobile, following protocol. **'Why the code-in David?'**

Harris ordered it . . . and besides it's our fucking job, you prick! Open up.'

The gates opened and Keegan drove in.

'You're not doing the mobile footage thing to compare images?' Cooney asked lethargically. 'Sara will have your balls, English!'

'I wish mate.'

Inside the house, the assassin eased his suppressed Browning away from Yakov Zorin's earlobe. 'Downstairs Spetsnaz . . . now!'

He had gained entry to Stanley Hall in the afternoon following the Sheikh's London intel and had shot the two Bengals as they slept in their exercise yard. He saw Assaf asleep in his cell but left him undisturbed. The house's perimeter sensors had been complicated to avoid but he had seen and evaded the exact same set-up in Dubai the previous summer when he had assassinated a Columbian minister for a cabinet rival. As the killer ushered the Russian into the basement, he called for him to halt outside Assaf's cell.

Assaf opened his sleepy eyes to the black clad figure holding a weapon to his Russian captor's head. 'Ha . . . shoot that Russian pig before he tries something.'

The killer was already waiting for Zorin's move, noticing his muscles tensing whenever he thought he had the slightest window of opportunity. He had earlier bound the Russian to an upstairs pillar but had sliced off the plasti-cuffs when the code-in call came through.

'Did the Sheikh send you, friend?'

A brief moment of confusion crossed the killer's features that provoked Zorin to spin around, but it was to no avail. The Browning's bullet smacked Yakov's head into the cell's bars and he crumpled to the ground.

'Yes! Get his keys my friend . . . his soldier pals can't be far away.'

'First of all, I have to make sure you are not a decoy,' the assassin said unhooking the keys from Zorin's belt. 'Tell me the Sheikh's exact location.'

'What?' Assaf answered stupefied, 'you know that is forbidden.'

A noise came from upstairs, followed by shouts of "Yakov" and "where are you Spetsnaz?"

'If you don't know, then I leave you here, imposter,' the contract killer remarked.

The Arab panicked, 'I know but I can't reveal it . . . you should know-'

The Browning jerked and the bullet caught the Arab in the sternum. Haroon Rashid Assaf had joined his wife in the afterlife.

'Yakov . . . Zorin?' Cooney shouted as he walked down the stairs.

'You fucking Russian Muppet, we could be a jihadist pizza delivery boy for all you could-'

Both men had reached the bottom step to see their Russian comrade's boots surrounded by a pool of black blood. Keegan gave Cooney the silent signal and pulled a Sig automatic from his waistband.

'Fuck!' Cooney mouthed upon discovery of the two corpses.

'Go upstairs and get a pump action and do a recce, Seamus. This is fresh . . . the intruder must be down there with the Bengals or out in the yard. Hurry man!'

It took both men just over twenty minutes to clear the house. The landline was now dead and Seamus had warned Keegan not to use his mobile until he had swept the entire house clean of IED presence.

'Where the fuck is Rebel?' Cooney asked as his colleague began to look for a trace of any disturbances.

'Haven't seen him mate but don't hold your breath. A man that kills two fucking Bengals wouldn't flinch with an Alsatian. Sorry, I didn't mean to-'

'Stop, don't move.'

Keegan froze like a statue as his hand touched the larder's door handle. 'What?'

'Move slowly back, English.'

The sweat trickled down Keegan's neck on hearing the intensity in the tone of the former IRA man's voice.

Look at the floor David!'

David looked down but could see nothing. 'You're giving me the shits here, Irish.'

There's moisture on it,' Seamus replied.

That sneaky callous bastard!' Keegan sighed with relief when Seamus eventually cut through the centre of the heavy door to see two trip wires attached to the slip-lock handle.

That tidy lot would have taken out part of Oxfordshire, my SAS friend!' Seamus said wiping his forehead with his sleeve.

There was a crate of C-4 explosives at their feet. Pulling the handle from outside the larder would have detonated the stash, sending the house down on top of them.

We had better get the fuck out of here, Irish. We have been well and truly compromised.'

Yeah, I'll call Harris now.'

Seamus walked from the larder to gain a signal. David walked over to the shelf of bottled water.

'Oh man . . . that is good,' he said cherishing the cooling liquid. 'Fuck . . . Seamus! I think I found Rebel?'

Cooney walked back in to see his colleague open one of the large refrigerators which had a small blood patch on the front panel.

'Don't!' The Irishman shouted in terror.

Keegan opened the lid and before he could focus on the lifeless dog inside, he saw the flash. The detonation followed, vaporising the men and blasting through the house, bringing down the central beams. The killer had set an initial ruse that he knew would be suspicious but had packed double the amount of C-4 into the refrigerator and placed the fallen Alsatian on top with a deliberate sign of blood. The detonator coil had been attached to the wire that was attached to the lid.

Passing motorists braked and bumped one another as debris flew in all directions. Stanley Hall looked as if it was sinking into a once lush meadow that now looked like a scorched earth scene from a war movie.

In Twickenham, Harris looked at his caller's display showing Cooney's number. After four attempted phone-backs, he stalled and called Bernard Jenkins.

## CHAPTER FOURTEEN

Jim Brannigan's hands and knees bore the cuts and bruises he had inflicted on himself when he had barged past the emergency services in search of his wife and child. Peters had driven him the short distance to Oxford Street and flashed his badge to access the cordoned off area. The bomb squad had warned them of further possible devices but Brannigan had ignored them. The Cobra committee had insisted that he stay with them but their pleas fell on deaf ears. Jim had already lost one wife and he felt that somehow his presence in the aftermath of the bomb would see his wife and son alive and well. His frantic desperation turned to utter horror when he came across items of familiar clothing and then a huddle of meshed bodies under a destroyed escalator. He threw off fire-fighters who were trying to warn him of nearby fires and crawled into the carnage before eventually blacking out. His world had been taken away, again.

**

The Prime Minister had paid Jim a visit in a secure room at the Charring Cross Hospital at eight in the evening. His heart was heavy; there had been fifty-seven fatalities in the Oxford Street and Kensington suicide attacks and a further two hundred people had suffered injuries, some life threatening. Peters accompanied the PM back to Downing Street where the remaining members of Cobra sat in sombre mood.

'How is Jim coping, sir?' The MI6 chief asked.

'It's hard to tell, he didn't say anything. Can you imagine it . . . what it feels like to lose your wife and child?'

'We won't see Jim again, he's a broken man.' Peters remarked as he took his chair.

'I thought his injuries were superficial?' The Home Secretary enquired.

'True Minister, but I was referring to his spirit.'

'Sad . . . so very sad,' Jenkins observed. 'But, we carry on gentlemen? I can confirm that the Oxfordshire explosion was an attack on our TFB unit. Two more have died and their base is in ruins.'

'Shit!' The Deputy PM said loudly. 'We now know that this whole terror plot is a coordinated attack by someone who knows the inner workings of our entire response capability?'

'We have been infiltrated gentlemen, of that I am certain.'

'Why so certain now, Bernard?' Asked the PM.

'Only a few people had knowledge of the unit's Oxfordshire base, sir. Before when the American sniper was killed, I was uncertain-'

'But now you think we have a mole at the heart of government?'

Absolutely, Prime Minster.' Jenkins responded.

As the meeting progressed and the screens updated the death toll from the day's atrocities, the PM began to think of an idea that he could share with just one man at the table - DCI Maurice Peters. Before the committee could deal with the fact that Feltham had been a decoy and there were other bombers at loose, he had to know that the investigation could progress unhindered by treachery. Peters was the only person he could trust, as he was the only outsider.

\*\*\*

Jim Brannigan checked himself out of the hospital, refusing the insistent demands of the protection detail of the four armed officers who had been assigned to protect him. He wanted to be at home, the only place he could mourn the loss of his family, alone. The officers eventually gave in after contacting the Commissioner through a Scotland Yard link. Jim's boss knew the man for so long, the way he thought and the way he would be feeling now. He ordered a mobile unit to station themselves near Brannigan's home in the North West London suburb of Kentish Town, a modest semi-detached affair within walking distance of his station.

Jim paid his taxi fare, put his key in the door and entered the gloom of a house that had been his oasis of serenity. He stood in the hall and looked about, remembering the laughter and the tears that the three of them had shared. If he had been his normal, alert self, he would have noticed that the alarm panel was left slightly ajar, something that Teresa never used to do. When the house alarm was in use, the panel would either be left open entirely or closed shut. His deadened senses also missed the noise of the back door closing with a soft click. The lounge's landline phone cradle had been deactivated, leaving just the kitchen and the upstairs phone capable of receiving a call.

\*\*\*

The Cobra suite burst into activity when the call came through from an MI6 unit in Feltham. A middle aged Arab, acting suspiciously, had returned a mobile phone after complaining that its camera function was faulty. He had been loud and argumentative. After swapping it for a newer device, he was followed to a nearby terraced house and the SAS standby unit called in. A fibre optic cable had been burrowed into the dimly lit dwelling; enough to see that the property was suspect. The last of the martyrs noticed the cable but carried on as though he had not, while preparing for his imminent death. He had served the Sheikh and believed he was leaving the world in a better place. His excursion to the telephone retail outlet had been deliberate; a stunt that was sure to trigger an alert as jihadists and taped martyrdom messages went hand in hand. The power was cut at 16 Malvern Place at precisely 11 p.m. just as a shape charge blew through the wall of the upstairs bedroom where Mufaddal Nassar, the last of the three-man terror cell, lay waiting. As the first SAS trooper entered the smoke filled room, Nassar thumbed a switch connecting his suicide vest to a cache of C-4, nitrate dispersed throughout the small dwelling. The Special Forces unit did not stand a chance as the building reared up from the ground and collapsed into rubble, taking down houses either side with it. The blast had been so intense that the underground sewage pipes had buckled and parts of the roof fell onto roads a mile from Malvern Place. Nassar had sent his martyrdom video message to the Al Jazeera broadcaster the very moment he saw the intrusive cable fed camera downstairs.

Once more, the elite members of the Cobra committee sat waiting for a screen to show them what they had sought to prevent. The unedited Nassar video showed him and his two fellow jihadists sitting cross-legged on the floor against a wall draped in a British Union flag. The three men spoke in adequate English, taking responsibility for the Heathrow airliner attack before claiming Oxford Street, Kensington and Feltham as acts that would awaken their fellow Jihadists into declaring a new holy war on the West. Their aim was very precise - the removal of all infidels from Moslem lands, Saudi Arabia most particularly.

No mention of Oxfordshire?' Jenkins remarked after a second viewing of the tape.

'It means only one thing Bernard. Assaf's body is believed to be among the ruins of the unit's Stanley Hall base so whoever perpetrated that attack is unconnected with Nassar and his cohort's deeds?' The MI5 chief proposed.

'Or wants us to think so. Assaf could have been collateral damage, a liability to-'

'This Sheikh character we have heard about but have no evidence of?' The PM butted in.

\*\*\*

The Saudi capital of Riyadh was in chaos as rivalling cousins sought the throne of their slain leader. The Sheikh at the heart of the mayhem waited in the wings while his rivals denounced each other and sought support from sections of the armed forces and the Mutaween, the feared religious police. He had already secured enough backing to march on the palace and proclaim his right to rule as he had had the foresight to do so. For years, the Saud clan had grown older with each branch of the family vying for favour with the late king. Succession in the kingdom was not as straightforward as outsiders had imagined. The Sheikh waited but as he did so, he sent an unprecedented four emergency messages to his contract assassin's dating inbox. The prerequisite Facebook novel 'liked' earlier had been Victor Hugo's 'Les Miserables' - an apt title considering the change of power about to happen in the oil rich kingdom that was up for grabs.

\*\*\*

153

Jim Brannigan cut a lonely figure as he sat in his lounge drinking red wine while watching homemade movies that Teresa had diligently edited throughout the lifespan of their son, John. From the aftermath of his birth, through to his first steps onto his first school sports day and a family holiday in Orlando - memories than stabbed at Jim's heart as he began glugging rather than drinking his third bottle of wine. His left hand was woven in a light bandage dressing, protecting the burns and cuts he had suffered crawling towards his family's remains. As he pressed reply once more of a scene showing Teresa holding her newborn son in St Mary's Hospital, Jim's telephone rang. He looked to the phone beside his favourite armchair, not bothering to reason why it was silent and the kitchens and upstairs handsets were working. He simply did not care anymore. All he had done since he got home was view a text message from DCI Peters about the Feltham destruction. He looked at it and switched off the device, not even bothering to switch to the news channel. He was numb. It took seven consecutive calls before he eventually arose and staggered to the kitchen where he fell but got to his feet in time to hear a voice -

**I know who killed your family. Come back in and talk to me?'**

What . . . who the fuck is this?'

The line went dead so he checked the last incoming call to see that it was a withheld number. He threw the handset across the kitchen in despair.

'Jim?'

He lurched back towards the lounge from where the voice had come from.

The assassin was standing in front of the closed back door that led out to the garden.

'Who the fuck are you?'

'Sit down, please.'

Brannigan was so drunk that despite the suppressed handgun pointing at him from a good fifteen feet away, he had thoughts of lunging forward. He paused to recall the words he had just head - *come back in and talk?*

'That was you on the phone just now?'

'Yes.' The killer answered gesturing to his armchair. 'Sit down, I haven't much time.'

Jim found himself sitting down for one reason only, the .38 Smith and Wesson revolver that he had stashed down the side of his chair's cushion. He had retrieved the gun from the attic when he had returned home, before he began drinking. The intruder kept his back to the rear door, partially hidden in shadow his face masked by a baseball cap pulled low.

I did not kill your wife and child. It is important that you know that and vital that you believe it.'

'Why?'

'I have taken lives recently but I am no bloodthirsty fanatic. There is a difference. I wouldn't want to live out my life not knowing who the real culprit was. I am innocent of their deaths and I want you to know that in the event that I ever become connected to the tragedy in the years ahead.'

Jim's mind was in a whirl of booze meddled despair and confusion. 'What are you talking about? Why break into my home and . . . and tell me something like that? *Who are you?*'

'I am the man who knows who killed your family. He is-'

'Some fucking Sheikh scum . . . yeah?'

The assassin presumed that Cobra had made some headway but was slightly surprised to hear the certainty in the officer's voice. 'He hired me to eliminate a group of people but events have taken place that sicken me. Do you know his actual name?'

'No.' Brannigan replied, intrigued enough to reach for his glass of wine. 'Nor do I know your name . . . who are you? Step forward into the light so I can see who in my home.'

'Switch over to any news channel,' the assassin said, 'and please don't mistake the remote control for that revolver you have wedged between your chair's cushion.'

'What . . . how. What the fuck is going on here?' Brannigan said as he picked up the remote to change the television to images of destruction beneath the breaking news banner of the Feltham terrorist attack. The news was relaying on all the major channels.

'I saw you through this window before I called you. You chambered one bullet Brannigan? Did you think that would be enough to face someone desperate enough to target you in your own home?'

Jim felt more alone than he could ever have possibly imagined. 'One bullet is all I need.' The evening was not going to plan. 'Are you that someone?'

'No,' the assassin replied curtly. 'I am the someone who is going to kill the man who murdered your wife and child today in Oxford Street. That's all you need to know really.'

'Feltham?' Jim asked watching the screen. 'Heathrow, Kensington . . . my family?'

'The Sheikh . . . the man who I am going to kill.'

For reasons unbeknown to him, Jim suddenly felt at ease. 'You must be this phantom contract killer I suppose. Mister Fucking Elusive . . . yeah?'

'I wanted you to know that I am innocent of your family's blood and had no prior knowledge of it. None.'

'And if you had of?'

'I would have stopped it-'

'You're a killer!'

The assassin watched in disbelief as the cop reached slowly and deliberately for his Smith and Wesson.

'Don't do it Brannigan. That wine won't dull the pain of a bullet in your kneecap.'

Jim closed his eyes and slowly placed the barrel of his revolver beneath his chin. As the intruder had made no move, he then reopened his eyes.

'I am in agony and I have no wish to live any longer. If I had tried to hit you with my one shot, you would have killed me . . . so allow me this.'

'What do you mean?'

'Can you kill this Sheikh . . . can you stop him and make him pay for what he as done?'

'It is my intention to do so.'

'That is what I thought. If what I have heard about this assassin . . . *you*, is even partially true then he would have a better chance than me and all of Cobra of killing this Arab.'

'That would be true but why the gun now? Surely you want to live to see justice done?'

The crack of the Smith and Wesson answered his question. Jim Brannigan's head jolted back as a spry of blood hit the wall. Peters' words had proven true - he was broken.

# CHAPTER FIFTEEN

The armed unit parked down the road from Jim's house had entered the property after calling for back-up. They had found their fellow officer's body and called again only to be diverted through to the Commissioner who informed his fellow Cobra members of another tragic death. The Prime Minster guided DCI Maurice Peters into his study on the pretence of discussing Brannigan's death. What he had to say shocked the habitually composed police officer.

'Are you positive about this, Prime Minster?'

'Sadly, I am. We have a leak and we have to be certain that at least Cobra is clean, so we start from the top, work our way down and catch this traitor.'

'That's a strong word, sir.'

'It is detective but what other word would suffice when it appears that someone is leaking our efforts to catching the mastermind behind the worst atrocities to hit Britain in generations. We are effectively at war Peters.'

'You're the boss.'

'Unfortunately I am. What will be required to weed out any informer from within our committee?'

'That's relatively simple sir. We set a trap . . . I will require the assistance of a chap I know who works at my station's forensics . . .'

The PM listened as Maurice outlined his plan, fascinated by its simplicity.

\*\*\*

The killer entered his South London abode, his mind fresh with the image of the cop's suicide. His Latchmere Road flat overlooking Lavender Hill Police Station was not as comfortable as his other home but it did have a few lively pubs and clubs nearby that he would sometimes frequent. His North London house opposite Brannigan's Kentish Town station was too close to increased police activity and the waiting media to spend the night in even though it was the favourite of his two addresses. He peeled off the prosthetic nose he had used and shook off the uncomfortable blond wig that had been covered by his cap. With one strand of blond hair showing, coupled with the nose, his tinted John Lennon glasses and khaki jacket, he had achieved the look of a man far removed from his reality. He had work to do, interpreting the Sheikh's seemingly urgent messages. After a warm bath and a delivered Hawaiian pizza and bottled spring water, he settled down at his laptop and went through the tedious task of decoding the messages.

'Les Miserables? The Arab wanker!'

As was his way, he switched the television on at its lowest volume setting but was immediately transfixed by another breaking news item. He switched from BBC to CNN to get a better perspective and turned up the sound.

' . . . to repeat, the president escaped injury but two of his secret service protection team did not survive the initial blast. Sources in Washington had earlier claimed that the first lady had been walking from Air Force One to the car when the Andrews Air Force base utility truck exploded but these reports have now been denied. Two of the attackers, believed to be of Middle Eastern origin, were killed by the blast and another was shot and killed by the secret service as he was about to detonate a suicide vest that ultimately failed to explode. Back to the studio for now . . ."

'The fucking madman,' remarked the Sheikh's hired killer. 'How many people was he involved?'

He turned down the television volume, wondering what Cobra would be making of the latest outrage and guessing also as to the number of contract killers the Sheikh had hired to attack the West. It seemed as if it was a continuous flow of bloodlust. Although aware of electronic footprints when dealing with the internet, he typed in the Saud royal family tree and clicked through several links before he came up with the face of the man who had hired him. It was his first time to do it as he never really troubled himself with contracted personal data or their reasons for his use, but this was different. Abdullah ibn Saud, a second cousin to the assassinated king, stared back at him from his laptop - the chubby faced pastry eater from the cave. He was intent on grabbing the oil rich state at any cost and that made him the most dangerous man that the killer had ever agreed terms with. Terms that were now redundant as he would not be following through with the remaining targets. He knew there would be a back-up in place and it was probably the Arab sounding man who telephoned with his intelligence updates. Who the intel caller was getting the updates from was a mystery but the mole had to be high level - maybe even a member of the Cobra committee itself. That was their worry. His initial plan would be to surreptitiously return the Sheikh's twenty five million and kill him in the process, retaining the money. As soon as the wave of terror subsided and the ports reopened, he would travel to Italy to organise the meeting and from there he would disappear forever; relocating to the Caribbean to live out his dream. Brannigan was a good man whose family had been dreadfully unlucky to be in Oxford Street, unlucky as all of the others at the other killing grounds. Except for the Sheikh and his personal guard, his days of killing would be confined to the past. Whether his conscience troubled him in old age was something he did not care to dwell on until the time came. He had one last thing to do, contact the Cobra unit's two survivors, the leader Harris and the Israeli woman, and inform them of the other three remaining targets he had been contracted to kill. Blanch the Prime Minister and the queen's son would have to be notified that their lives were in danger. He would ruminate over that later; firstly, he had the Sheikh' messages. It took him longer than normal to decode the ramblings as his ear was attentive to the updating CNN Washington broadcast but eventually he grasped he general mood of the Sheikh - he wanted to know why his targets had not been eliminated, especially the Prime Minister of Great Britain. The assassin had no time whatsoever for any politician as he viewed them all with distaste, using their armed forces to garner votes when the public grew weary of them. Nevertheless, Blanch, the PM and the prince had to be alerted and he would not be doing that himself. He would alert Harris and the Mossad woman and it would be their duty to warn the others. He himself would be extra cautious from now on as there was something in the Arab intel messenger's voice that made him slightly edgy. He couldn't tell what it was but there was a gravity to it, a confidence that said - this is what you do and don't fail us. The edginess came from the fact that he didn't know who the man was or where he was. If he knew, he would take him out immediately, no questions asked. Then it dawned on him that he might be able to use Harris and kill the two birds with one stone - metaphorically speaking. The unit leader would have to make contact with his benefactor and hopefully it would be a meeting, and the lord of the realm was someone whose itinerary he knew well.

**

Hakim Nassar, the brother of Mufaddal Nassar, the Feltham suicide bomber sat watching Al Jazeera's Washington broadcast in the dining room of the Westminster flat he had bought three years previously. Unlike his dead brother, Hakim was no wild-eyed fanatic who contented himself into the afterlife by killing a few infidels via a vest. He was a callous killer who had murdered indiscriminately for the Saudi religious police and he was the Sheikh's loyal servant. At six foot two and broad shouldered, he was an awesome spectacle to behold when seen training or even in the gyms that he used to attend before the terror campaign began. He was a sleeper, a man waiting in the wings. The Sheikh had tasked him with passing intelligence from his UK government contact onto the infidel assassin before finally eliminating the killer when his purpose had expired. He cared not for the twenty five million that had been paid and Hakim would not be paid one Saudi riyal beyond his expenses. His currency was loyalty to the Sheikh who believed him to be better at killing than the foreigner he had hired. The Westerner had been hired because he was precisely that - male Caucasian and able to blend in. The Saudi royal was wary of the infidel as his reputation demanded, but deemed him no match for Hakim who was totally ruthless. A contract killer who killed for money was one thing, a killer who killed for pleasure while carrying out his duties was quite another and Hakim shared his mentor's vision of a new, independent, powerful Saudi Arabia. Although of pure Saudi blood, Hakim did have the advantage of fairer than normal skin and hair tone and could affect a variety of Western accent from English upper class to London Cockney and his Louisiana drawl matched his privileged Harvard enunciation. With the correct amount of cosmetic applied, the callous killer could pass for a Westerner in the right circumstances

The Sheikh's henchman watched the news and once more checked his weaponry while delving through a multitude of scenarios that would lead him to kill the infidel assassin after he completed his final contract. It was a waiting game, waiting for the next piece of intelligence from the Cobra committee who the Sheikh had bought and paid for in anticipation of his attempt to seize power of one of the world's wealthiest nations. Blanch and the prince were headline targets but the Prime Minister's death would play right into the Sheikh's hands as he had a ready-made scapegoat - the foreign assassin whose subsequent death would tie off any evidence of Saudi involvement. Hakim smiled at the image of the frail Vice President making a speech from the White House press office, knowing that the failed attempt on his leader's life and the impending death of the British leader would occupy them for years to come, distracting them from the Saudi succession crisis. More importantly, the communications delivered to the infidel killer and the diamonds would be seen as emanating from Iran, a country the Sheikh despised.

**

The tension in the Cobra suite was beginning to boil over after the Prime Minister had returned from Parliament where he had endured an uglier than normal exchange with the leader of the Labour opposition. Initially, they had been supportive and had gathered round to portray a unified defiance but since the post Heathrow attacks, the government had come under pressure from the media, and Labour had taken the opportunity to add fuel to the fire, sighting the government's weakness as a weapon in the next general election. Terrorism was terrorism but politics was politics. To add to the governments woes, fringe elements such as the UKIP party newcomers were whipping up public fervour in the media with their anti-immigration agenda. Thuggish behaviour by the English Defence League and other disreputable mobs had begun to tax the police's already stretched resources while the social network sites were crashing repeatedly due to the unprecedented crisis. The attack on his US counterpart had astounded the Prime Minister, rendering him insecure and brittle, and in his more private moments - genuinely scared of the rapid and continuing use of violence in the supposed new world order. The catastrophic 9/11 attacks had been shocking but confined to the United States and to a single morning whereas recent events pointed to a global apocalyptic scenario that showed no signs of stalling. It was no longer a question of "if we got hit but when we got hit" and how bad would it be.

The PM wasted no time. 'I want to know how the Feltham terror cell managed to split into three, enabling them to bomb Oxford Street and Kensington while we sat here. It's a simple fucking question and I demand a straightforward answer . . . right the fuck now if you please!'

Bernard Jenkins watched his colleagues shift in their comfortable leather seats. He had spoken to the PM on the way back from the House of Commons assuring him that Oxfordshire was a different ball game; the work of someone else who wanted the Cobra denial unit neutralised. The phantom assassin loomed large in the Prime Minster's thoughts but if the Sheikh wanted a free reign of terror in Britain, why target them, when the entire police and military infrastructure of the country was at Cobra's disposal. There was something dramatically wrong with the scope of things and the unknown Sheikh had obviously perceived the denial unit as the main threat to his terror campaign. Both men were satisfied that it was no ordinary government figure, aide or even a junior minister who had blabbed innocently to a friend or lover. The unit was Cobra classified, meaning the leak must be within Cobra. As Jenkins and the PM were driven the short distance to Downing Street that morning they knew intuitively that their fears were based on facts, though both men still found the whole idea too surreal to dwell upon.

"It would be like Colonel Sanders switching to Kentucky Fried Rat, I just can't fathom a reason for a Cobra member to rat on us." Jenkins had said in an attempt to cheer his disillusioned leader.

**CHAPTER SIXTEEN**

The anonymous assassin had spent some time watching Sir Raymond Blanch and had done as much research as the internet would allow into the private life of the celebrated businessman and Lord of the realm. As he watched the darkness slowly descend outside his home, his television attention began to wane of the US presidential attack that was now repeating the news without further updates, his thoughts turned to the evening's fundraising event in the city's Mansion House. No doubt the politicians would have already sent their apologies and would not attend but Blanch would be there due to his passionate support in the fight against the Ebola outbreak in West Africa. The only question was - would Harris have made arrangements to meet him before the cameras turned up or afterwards at the mogul's London home? As had often happened in the past, a plan slowly formulated that became more positive as it spiralled through his mind. He opened a carton containing a new pay-as-you-go mobile phone. As he connected the charger to the wall socket, his exclusive Sheikh alone mobile beeped - withheld number showing.

'Hello?'

**'Blanch, no show Mansion House tonight. Venue and time changed to National Theatre at noon tomorrow due to increased security. Repeat Blanch attending National Theatre fundraising event, tomorrow noon. Sheikh unhappy with-'**

He cancelled the call, as he knew that a straightforward attempt at interrupting or engaging the gravel voiced Arab in conversation would ultimately fail once the intel had been delivered. He was bluffing, depending on the caller to phone back, which he did after two anxious minutes. This time he was ready.

Tell the Sheikh that our agreement-'

This time, the Arab hung up and it was another anxious two minutes before he called back. Once again, the killer did not give the messenger time to deliver his message.

Tell the Sheikh that our arrangement . . . ' The line was silent so he asked, 'are you still there?'

Yes.'

Good, so listen carefully, Harris and the Israeli have gone to ground so I will need help in finding them. Still there?'

Continue.'

Can you be of help to me . . . or can anyone else of the Sheikh's followers?'

 cannot.'

Why not, it's a two man job and if your boss wants this contract fulfilled I will need assistance distracting Harris and the woman.'

**'Give me an hour.'**

Before he had the chance to answer, the line went dead.

Two hours passed without the Arab calling back so the assassin cleared his mind and switched channels to watch a television movie punctuated by tedious advertisements.

\*\*\*

The Prime Minister breezed into the Cobra suite and motioned to an aide carrying a supermarket style basket.

'Gentlemen, your attention.'

All eyes were on the aide and the basket, rather than the PM.

'All of us are going to place our personal mobile devices, including tablets and such, into personal envelopes and place them into that basket during these debriefings.'

The MI6 and MI5 chiefs could hardly contain their annoyance as they knew th implications of such an unheralded request. Everyone else merely looked to what the person beside them was thinking of doing.

'But Prime Minister . . . what if the unit's remaining members have somethin vital for us? These meetings can last hours-'

When I said everyone Bernard, I meant everyone, you included.'

Of course, Prime Minister.'

The rumblings continued as each man signed an envelope containing their mobiles and placed them into the basket. To the surprise of everyone in attendance, the PM signed his and placed it among the others. The MI6 head and his MI5 counterpart suddenly rethought their misgivings.

The obvious question, Prime Minister, is why?' Asked the ever curious Home Secretary.

That is simple. The technical wizards at GCHQ have suggested that our meetings have been compromised so if any of our communication devices have been bugged, they won't know of tonight's briefing.'

The Deputy Prime Minister stood up. 'Well I for one will openly state that I cannot agree to this violation of our privacy. It's a bloody outrage and hints at disloyalty at best.'

As you wish, but when you leave here tonight, it will be for the last time. You can summon a junior minister in your stead, if that is your wish.'

As the Deputy PM reached the exit, he paused. 'Okay, one question Prime Minister, if I may?'

Ask it?'

'Are we to infer that while we sit here doing our level best to end this nightmare, our personal phones are to be trawled through by some technophiles from GCHQ or some other agency?'

'Absolutely not Nick, that was never my intention, though we should all avail of a personal hands-on bug sweep while not in Cobra attendance. I am having my own phone looked at in the morning.'

'Oh well, that's different . . . and now I suppose that all your attention will be focused on my behaviour just now?'

'Not in the slightest. Now let's get some tea and coffee sent in and get down to sorting out this mess.'

'How the Feltham bombers split up into three, sir?' Peters replied instantly knowing the full reason for the phone basket.

'Precisely detective!'

\*\*\*

The killer's phone buzzed as the movie came to a predicable end. He didn' mind poorly scripted films as much as the next person as they gave his mind a chance to breathe when a scene would make no sense or a line of dialogue wa delivered ineptly.

'Hello?'

'What exactly do you need me to do tomorrow?'

'I need you inside the National Theatre tomorrow at noon and to text this phone ten seconds before Blanch reaches either the side exit or front exit.'

'Why?'

'I will have my scope on him but cannot expose my position for too long as I would definitely be spotted by the security services. They will probably have a helo in the air if I'm not wrong.'

'I cannot be involved. It is impossible.'

'Then the Sheikh will have to bide his time. I told him at the cave that I do not place myself in harm's way and I meant that.'

'Give me one minute?'

'I will but I would have thought that the Sheikh with his connections could arrange for you . . . or someone who knows our plans to attend an event like-'

The line went dead again.

'Pleasant fucker, aren't you!' The assassin mused as his thoughts turned to his Caribbean retirement.

Ten minutes later, the gravel voiced messenger phoned back.    'I will text you you have suggested. Do not let us down.'

The line went dead.

'I won't let you down pal, I will drop you when I catch up with you.' The killer mused as he lay back on his couch and thought out his plan. His aim would have to be sharp and he would have to be quick but that was his mantle. His last hits would be kills that he might even enjoy, something to soothe a troubled conscience in retirement.

# CHAPTER SEVENTEEN

DCI Maurice Peters stood beside the bank of screens in the Cobra suite, most of which displayed maps of Feltham and possible routes leading to Central London.

'There are a number of possibilities as to how the terror cell fractured but before I continue, can we all agree that the Feltham bomber, Nassar, was a deliberate ploy to keep us focussed on the Feltham area?'

There was a murmur of consent around the table, the PM nodded, knowing that Peters was using the essential briefing to allow his forensics colleague to conduct a more essential exercise.

'How did the two bombers get from Feltham to Oxford Street and Kensington? Thirteen and eleven miles respectively?' Peters motioned to the MI5 chief who stood and joined him at the electronic wall.

'We have searched through countless hours of CCTV footage and found no signs of the two bombers using public transport and we must assume that they could not have taken their chances in a car.'

Peters thanked the spook and resumed the briefing. As he was doing so, his forensics pal from Saville Row police station was sitting at the Prime Minister's computer in his private office. Ted Nugent was old school but he had caught up with the Met's younger computer whizz kids as the need demanded and he found himself enjoying what he had thought would be a nightmare. Peters' plan had been simple but it all depended on whether a mole would take the chance.

Peters meanwhile, was in his zone. He was now familiar with the array of Cobra screens and the remote to use them.

'Instead of looking at Feltham and the routes into London, I have backtracked with the help of MI5, and we have identified the bombers entering their London targets. We more or less followed them backwards gentlemen.'

'They walked those distances, Peters?' The Foreign Secretary asked.

'Correct sir, look at these images.' Peters used a speeded relay from one screen to another until he had the two hooded figures leaving Malvern Place where Nassar had detonated his cache of explosives.

'Fuck me!' The Foreign Office representative remarked. 'Simple as that . . . they walked all that way wearing shitloads of explosives! Well I never would have imagined that detective.'

'What if they had been stopped or reported as suspicious along the way Peters' The PM enquired though knowing the answer.

'They would simply have detonated near the most desirable target they deemed appropriate to keep us occupied, sir.'

Well I'll be damned,' the Home Secretary added. 'And your reasoning behind this, detective?'

If someone wants to distract us and is already convinced of seventy virgins then it was down to how far they would get, Home Secretary. How much damage they could inflict.'

And unfortunately for us, they managed to get all the way to their targets.' The Deputy PM observed.

Okay,' the PM announced. 'I am now of the mind that what the CIA think is probably near the mark.'

An even bigger threat you mean, Prime Minister?'

Yes Bernard, everything was a diversion for the man who the CIA believe to be his phantom assassin, the needle in the haystack fucker.'

Wow!' The Deputy PM replied. 'Seriously?'

'm all ears if anyone has an alternative. Look at what the terror cells have done
so far, add our unit's interrogation of Assaf who mentioned a mysterious Sheikh and what do you get?'

A conspiracy theory Prime Minister?' The PM's deputy replied with a half-hearted grin.

'I believe that there is someone out there waiting . . . whether it's an unknown assassin or not . . . is anyone's guess, but I believe there is.' The lowest ranking member said in an authoritative tone.

'I would have thought you too *analytical* for that Peters?' The MI6 man observed.

'Why not sir? What other scenario makes sense when you throw in the terror attacks in the States and Saudi?'

'Hmm,' the Deputy PM said, his face that of a poker player playing a bad hand. 'Let me think about that while I use the bathroom.'

'Shall we break for something to eat Prime Minister?' Jenkins enquired.

'No Bernard. We'll continue to think this through and grab some food later.'

As the session progressed, most of the committee found an excuse to leave the suite - some for the bathroom, others for a breath of fresh air and two for a nicotine fix.

'So we are now looking for a person, or persons unknown who might have killed a low level MI6 analyst and made it look like a burglary. If we believe the CIA . . . we are hunting a mythical contract killer who might be in the employ of a Sheikh who we have no name for. Correct?' The Home Secretary said, his gaze firmly on his boss at the end of the table.

Yep, that's about right.' The PM replied as he stood up to bring the debriefing to close.

Peters dawdled as the committee members slowly exited the room.

Are you tired, detective?'

No chance Prime Minister, I'm excited.'

The two men walked to the PM's office checking that all of the doors along the route had remained locked as per their instructions. All phone lines had been temporary cut while the committee had been in session.

Well Peters, did someone use it?' The PM enquired eagerly as his personal secretary arrived with a disc that would show anyone entering his office since the forensics expert had left the ultra violet detection dust on the computer's keyboard.

The room darkened, Peters used a strobe to examine the keyboard.

Bingo!' The DCI replied. 'Now let's look at the footage of who was in here, sir?'

The tape turned out to be a dud, the office camera had been switched off.

What the fuck!' The PM demanded as he gave the order for all Cobra committee members to return to the suite immediately.

'Gentlemen . . . someone here used my computer to send an email when we were in session earlier.'

The tired looking group looked perplexed. Nobody wanted to speak first so Peters had his say.

'With the Prime Minister's permission, I am going to pass each of you a cloth to wipe your fingers with.' He opened a small package and passed them out individually.

The Prime Minister of Great Britain was furious but was biding his time, as his outraged colleagues demanded an explanation.

'If anyone here refuses Peters instruction, that person will be detained for questioning.'

Gradually, each member wiped both hands with a cloth and placed it on the desk before them. More than one was ashen faced at the late night manoeuvrings of their superior. Peters dimmed the suites lights to adequately examine each cloth.

It took all of ten minutes to find that there was no evidence of any dye on any of the cloths. The PM looked vacantly at DCI Maurice Peters.

Outburst followed outburst as more than one member threatened resignation. The PM stood his ground and spoke to Peters when the shaken committee finally left Downing Street in the waiting fleet of government cars.

'Well, did it work Peters?'

'We got him, Prime Minister!' The DCI replied as he used a forensic brush to examine the leather chair that had been wiped clean earlier and pushed up against the computer desk. There were a set of fingerprints on the arm and headrest of the chair. The pencil used by the mole to tap out the email lay exactly in the spot where Peters had left it and the mole had memorised, to replace it beside the computer's smudged keyboard in the same position.

'And now we use the fucker!'

'Correct sir! To pass on crap information and nail this Sheikh.'

'Do you take a drink Maurice?' The PM asked with a sigh of relief.

'On an occasion as bizarre as this one, why not. A drop of brandy if you have it, sir?' Peters responded with an even bigger sigh.

The unorthodox detective had planned for all outcomes and catching a possible mole would only send any cohort, or cohorts underground. The traitor had to believe that he had passed the test and was in a position to carry on with his betrayal.

'Read out the email again Maurice? I can't believe the fucker had the cheek to use my email address and try to delete all sent messages.'

'He had to sir as time demanded and he would hardly have opened his own email on this computer. Your email account was open and the easiest option. You would be surprised what people think they can get away with. As Hitler said, the bigger the deception, the more people would believe in it-'

'I think it was Goebbels who said that but I do get what you are saying. He relied on us thinking,' the PM yawned and stretched, 'who would dare look at my personal email account?'

'Precisely.'

'Anyway, the email transcripts?'

'Here goes sir, **"Cobra aware of diversionary tactics, confirmed 23:15 UK time. Now tasked with finding Diamond assassin who they believe to be main threat. Warning advised."** As we thought, a contract killer who they are referring to as Diamond.'

'And the addressee Maurice?'

'It reads diam1274@gmail.com which will prove useless to us until GCHQ get their hands on it and try to find the 273 previous messages.'

'What?'

The email address is a one-off in my opinion and I doubt if he has sent 1,274 mails so I'm guessing the tech boys in Cheltenham will dismiss the first digit "one" and find evidence of 274 messages . . . I mean emails, sent up to, and including tonight.'

Will GCHQ be able to do that?'

I would think so sir, wouldn't you?'

You are driving up there tomorrow Maurice and you will stand over whoever is tasked with unravelling those emails. I will phone the director in Cheltenham as you are approaching the complex and not before.'

I'm driving to Cheltenham's GCHQ, sir?'

Yes Maurice. This is a fucked up scenario but trusting people has now become an issue. Are you up for it, detective?'

Are you kidding sir. I'll drive up the A40 tonight if you say it.'

No, you need rest. Meantime, let's drink to a fallen comrade.'

To Jim Brannigan!' Peters echoed as the pair clinked glasses in the early hours of the Downing Street night.

## CHAPTER EIGHTEEN

Approximately one third of a mile from London's National Theatre there was an apartment block that boasted a mixed bag of residents, from bankers to celebrities, to the few lucky ones who had owned an apartment before a major refurbishment had taken place. The assassin had sparked an earlier fire alert by placing a smoke bomb in the nearby BFI IMAX cinema's toilets. A crowd of people stood behind barricades, most of them cinema goers, some local residents and the mandatory curious onlookers. He had waited until the initial chaos had died down and then quizzed the apartment block's concierge as to the occupancy of the apartments. One couple who occupied the apartment beneath the penthouse were holidaying in India. It was their opulent abode that the killer had entered in his fire inspector's uniform and helmet, complete with a bushy moustache and clear glassed spectacles. He stood back from the wide open balcony after taping the curtains together to prevent them from appearing to rustle in the wind. From a distance, it was difficult to tell if the balcony doors were entirely open or firmly shut.

He glanced at his phone on the table that he used to balance his .243 Winchester rifle with the aid of a small stool and a cushion. The task ahead had no need for his favoured McMillan TAC .338. He had one other tool, a long range Olympus camera. As noon approached, he removed his helmet and set his shoulder to the butt of his weapon. Roughly 530 metres separated him from the theatre's exit

30 metres with a wind factor that would be irrelevant considering the descent of the shot.

As the killer adjusted his scope, a few early birds started to leave the theatre's front exit. A police helicopter banked over the Thames, part of the large scale security operation in process.

The killer's phone vibrated - ***Blanch headed to SIDE exit, approx 15 to 10 seconds.*** He glanced up from the text and saw the tycoon walk out to a positioned limousine by a line of bollards. Three private security men and two uniformed police officers kept the paparazzi and the curious at bay as they ushered the brochure carrying Blanch forward. The killer could make out the wording on the fundraising brochure. He tilted his aim and sent the tycoon spiralling to the ground with a bullet in his shoulder. The killer grabbed his camera and counted down the seconds before he saw a man emerge from the theatre, and then stop to use his mobile phone. He was suspect number one even though he didn't look like a typical Arab; it was the deadpan face and the way he glanced up and around at the taller of the buildings in sight. The killer tracked the man as he walked across Waterloo Bridge towards Westminster, observing him through his rifle's scope. The man stopped midway across to turn and look out over the river Thames, and to use his phone again. The killer's mobile vibrated seconds later - ***You fool, Blanch is not dead.***

'You don't say pal,' the assassin said to himself. 'You can share a bedpan with Blanch in that case!'

The bullet boomed from the Winchester's barrel and dug itself into the buttocks of the man gazing down onto the murky water below. Hakim Nassar was in need of emergency treatment. Passersby looked about them, unable to understand how the man had suddenly fallen over in a heap. Within a short time, Hakim was taken by ambulance to St Thomas' Hospital off Westminster Bridge, a few minutes away from where he had collapsed. The same hospital where Sir Raymond Blanch was having a bullet removed from his shoulder.

The killer grabbed his gear and thought through what he had just done, as it was an unreal experience for him. He had looked through his scope on so many occasions before squeezing his trigger to end people's lives. He had planted lethal devices and had killed people in close quarter combat but aiming to wound had sent a shiver through him. For the very first time, the assassin realised that he truly did possess a conscience and that killing people for reward was something near demonic. He had killed people on nearly every continent, some of them monsters who had themselves murdered thousands, like a Somali warlord he had dispatched for a relatively small sum two years previously. He had poisoned a British recording artist who had been responsible for numerous attacks on children over a two-year period. But he had also cut the throat of a priest in Mexico who had turned out to be innocent and had been set up by the lient. As he made his way home, he promised himself that he would seek out a ounsellor of some kind to talk it through; nothing to do with assassinations or ersonal issues but conscience in general.

**

Vow! This is some impressive place you have here, sir.' DCI Maurice Peters ommented to the director of the UK's ear-dropping surveillance facility that as Cheltenham's GCHQ - General Communications Headquarters.

he detective had been bowled over when arriving at the outskirts to the huge ase that employed over 6,000 people, quite a few who had parked their cars in ie endless spaces allocated around the architecturally imposing glass façade. e had earlier Googled GCHQ to see the aerial view of the recently constructed complex. It was known as "The Doughnut" because it had the 1ape of a doughnut from above. Beforehand, he had always imagined GCHQ be akin to a country estate building as in the old Enigma code-breaking ovies.

hank you, Detective Peters. All the Prime Minister has asked for is waiting for 1u in section D. I will take you there myself . . . top priority and hush-hush, I ar?'

hat it is, sir.'

Peters was amazed by the scale of the place even before he phoned the PM to tell him he was driving up to the sentry guarded gate. It was a city unto itself. The Prime Minister had seen to it that he was accorded "every ounce of effort and technical assistance" required as a matter of national urgency. GCHQ was on its toes.

Peters found himself sitting alongside a middle-aged man named Andrew who wore a neat brown beard. He had the look of a wizard even if you had seen him on the street.

'Are you a computer genius, Andrew?' Peters asked, shaking the outwardly geeky man's hand. *Would he be offended to be described as outwardly geeky?*

'Let's find out, Detective Chief Inspector Peters?'

'Please, I'm just Maurice. Now, can we grab a coffee while we work?'

'Eh . . . no sir. Sorry, no Maurice . . . no liquids are allowed in here. Would you like a quick trip to the canteen?' Andrew responded, looking over the shabby looking officer. *Would he be offended by shabby?* The spook mused, thinking of television's Columbo.

'Not to mind. Here is an email account,' Peters handed him a folded A4 sheet with one typed sentence. 'I would like to know Andrew if there were similar

nails sent from a variation of this emails number digits such as
am1271@gmail.com or diam1263@gmail.com and so on?'

he code breaker looked at the copper with a blank expression on his face, 'is
at it?'

es.'

h . . . okay.'

ou seem surprised Andrew, anything wrong?'

o, No Maurice. I was expecting something . . . something different.'

ow different?'

omething tricky?'

you,' Peters paused when Andrew stared blankly once more. '*When* you find
em, will you be able to tell me what the emails contained?'

ndrew didn't bother with the blank stare. His fingers worked like that of a
ncert pianist as they danced across the keyboard. His screen sprang into life,
ompting him to fold his arms. 'There you go Maurice.'

ters leant into the screen. '274 possible matches of data requested.'

es sir, I mean yes Maurice. I simply ran a search and now it is collating the
ails contents.'

'Thanks Andrew. The destination of the emails and the sender's computer IP and physical address?'

The concert pianist fingers performed an encore that made Peters momentarily wish that the task had been more difficult.

'You guys are amazing Andrew; it freaks me out to see how fast something can be done. Can I get a printout of everything you have provided and also the details on disk?'

'No problem Maurice, it's been a pleasure. Still want a coffee?'

DCI Maurice looked at his watch, reflecting on the fact that he had phoned ahead to book a room in a Cheltenham hotel for the night. The task had been secret so he could not have asked in advance as to the time it would take to accomplish it. Now, he would drink his coffee and drive back to London.

'A coffee sounds good Andrew. What's the food like in your canteen?'

'It's not great I'm afraid. What do you expect of Star Trek food though, ha?'

'Star Trek food?'

'Yes Maurice, like in Star Trek . . . the Next Generation? Where you speak to a computer replicator that provides you with a thousand choice variety and a meal in seconds?'

uck off!' Peters jibed as he eventually saw the grin broaden on Andrew's face. ut, it had taken a few seconds of the blank stare that had Peters picturing aptain Jean Luc Picard ordering a steak with all the trimmings.

otcha!'

et's grab that coffee, Andrew.'

\*

ere were more security personnel in St Thomas Hospital than there were tients. It was in essence a training facility but it did deal with emergency care. Raymond Blanch was in another theatre, the operating kind where a surgeon end had rushed to his aid. After a forty-minute procedure under general aesthetic, the small calibre round had been removed and the wound cleaned d shut. In an adjacent theatre, Hakim Nassar was still undergoing a delicate eration to have his buttock injury cleaned up. The slug had dug deeper than ginally thought causing a significant amount of tissue damage. A firearms t stood by in the corridor after the ambulance paramedics had reported a nshot wound from the bridge. The Sheikh's loyal assassin would be going where soon.

## CHAPTER NINETEEN

'The emails derived from different computer IP addresses and from all over the Middle East, Prime Minister. A few from Saudi Arabia, some from Yemen and Syria, but a large portion from Iran.'

'Shit!' The PM announced, handing DCI Maurice Peters a mug of scented India tea. He sipped his own and dwelled on the dreaded word - Iran.

'Our mole used his own personal computer mostly, which is idiotic if you think of it, sir.'

'Not so idiotic Maurice. He obviously believed he was above suspicion and that no one would ever look.'

'He sent this email message to diam1273@gmail.com just before our ploy snare him went live, sir.' Peters said as they sat in the living quarters of Ten Downing Street. Once again, the humble detective was overawed by the location as the PM leaned over him to view the laptop screen.

*'I have alerted Hakim. Blanch will not be at the Mansion House tonight. The venue and time have been changed to the National Theatre, London SE tomorrow at noon. Expect a lot of security.'*

'The traitorous fucker. He'll get a minimum of thirty years for his betrayal. Lucky the death sentence is no longer a punishment or he would swing for it.'

'Do you really think he'll see the inside of a cell, Prime Minster?'

The PM looked suddenly pale. 'Oh, I see,' he flustered. 'Well, there will be people who will want to avoid a trial-'

'The trial of the century sir!'

'Yes, yes . . . I understand where you are going with this. But right now, I am trying to estimate the total loss of life, the critically injured and the maimed that Jenkins is responsible for. Why?'

'Money?'

'What were you saying about this other man that got shot today on the bridge Maurice . . . a connection?'

'Absolutely sir, ballistics matched them to the same weapon.'

'Who is he again?'

'He is claiming diplomatic immunity under the name,' Peters checked his small black notepad. 'Khuram Abboud.'

'Have you checked with the Foreign Office if that is a bona fide name? Is he a genuine diplomat or a-'

'A spy or an agent, sir?'

'Yes Maurice, exactly.'

'No sir, not yet. I didn't know how close to home you were going to play this out. Could there be someone at the Foreign Office who might tip Jenkins off?'

'Do you fancy a trip over to St Thomas Hospital?'

'With you, sir?'

'No, I didn't mean that. I thought you might want to have a poke around . . . do your thing?'

'Is Sir Raymond Blanch the wealthy benefactor who organized the 'black' unit you used, Prime Minister?'

The PM stood up with his tea and paced the soft pile carpet. 'I trusted Jenkins and he betrayed me . . . betrayed everyone-'

'So you are wondering if you can trust me or if indeed I even need to know this information, sir?'

'Precisely.'

'You should, and you *can* trust me Prime Minister. I have signed the official secrets act and you also have my word that I will never mention it to anyone without your express permission. My word on it.'

'Blanch paid for the Task Force Black unit.'

'Thank you for the trust sir. Now, why was Blanch a target?'

A gentle knock disturbed their thoughts as the PM's wife entered the room carrying a tray of something aromatic. 'I thought I'd fix you something to eat.'

Her husband pecked her on the cheek as he accepted the tray. Peters looked on at the surreal image, recalling the sausage roll and bag of Nachos he had eaten last week in his station's canteen. He stood up.

'Thank you, Ma'am.'

'You are most welcome, detective. There are pears and ice cream for afterwards you have the same sweet tooth as this guy.'

'You are very kind,' Peters replied, watching the couple interacting.

'To think that Sir Raymond Blanch could have been shot dead today on the streets of our capital,' the PM remarked as they ate. 'The Prince of Wales would have thrown a fit!'

'Are they buddies?'

'You are an unusual man Maurice, a clever man. When this is all over, you are welcome to a posting in the security services if you would care to.'

'Thank you, sir, but I like being a copper.'

'Very unusual man. Let's look through the other emails. Are you enjoying that?'

'I am sir, delicious. What is it?'

The Prime Minister croaked with laughter. 'What?'

'Are you okay sir?'

'I am but do you know that this is the first time I have laughed since the firs Heathrow attack?'

'Oh?'

'My wife will be *thrilled* to hear that someone doesn't recognise her "infamous Hungarian Goulash. She assumes everyone is capable of knowing it by taste.'

Peters stopped chewing. 'But I do recognise delicious, sir.'

'Seriously?'

'It beats sausage rolls and kebabs!'

The PM wiped his mouth. 'I will have to let Blanch know that he is in dange Maurice. He had better go to ground until this is resolved, yes?'

'You think the gunman wanted Blanch dead sir?'

'Eh, yes . . . he got shot?'

'Do you remember your American sniper from the unit who was shot in the hea at the dog track?'

'Shit for bricks!'

'xactly sir. If this unknown . . . killer, wanted Blanch dead, he wouldn't be in
Thomas, he'd be in the morgue.'

'o you are telling me that it was the same man?'

'hen nothing else seems certain, it's not unwise to speculate. However, there is
ie anomaly sir, the weapons he used.'

'o on.'

'our unit's American took a headshot from a Magnum Lapua, designed to
'stroy. The weapon today seems to be a .243 Winchester system that provides
e same accuracy but is not heavy duty.'

'ɔ you are saying it was his intention to wound, not kill?'

'bsolutely sir.'

'nd this Saudi diplomat?'

'ie sniper shot him in the-'

'ss!'

'es sir and that tells me that instead of killing him, he wanted attention drawn
'him, in relation to what happened to Blanch.'

'ie ballistics and the location from the bridge to the theatre?'

'Exactly sir. I'm quite certain that the theatre's cameras will show the ma attending the Ebola fundraiser.'

'How would he have got an invite to that, it was tightly vetted.'

'A Saudi with diplomatic credentials?'

'Hmm.'

'It's a conundrum sir and as weird as it seems, this killer has given us a clue.'

'You are going to the hospital Maurice.'

'Don't tell your wife that it was her Goulash though, Prime Minister?'

The PM stared through the detective and laughed once more. For the first tim since the bombings had begun, he actually thought that there was an end in sig to the crisis that he would be forever remembered for. As his wife entered wi their desert, he mulled over the thoughts and whereabouts of Jenkins' remainir TFB unit members.

'What did you make of the GCHQ technophobes, Detective Peters?'

'They have a great sense of humour Ma'am. One guy mentioned a Star Tr food replicator in their canteen.'

'Oh goodness,' she said laughing, 'did you hear what they did to my hubby?'

eters waited for the PM to reveal the prank, which he duly did. 'My first time own in Cheltenham, I was introduced to some of the staff by the director and s I shook one of the chap's hand, he said "so you'll be wanting to see the aliens en Prime Minister?" but I told him that I see them all the time opposite me in e Commons.'

ice one, sir.' The cop smiled though he didn't think it that amusing.

suppose they have to have a sense of humour doing a job like theirs,' the PM's ife observed.

peak to Blanch, Maurice. I will need a meeting with Harris and the other rviving unit member.' The PM suggested after his wife had left them.

that wise sir?'

ell considering that Jenkins is implicated in the deaths of four of their lleagues, Harris will be totally at sea.'

agree sir that this Harris and the former Mossad woman need to be advised, t it can't be you . . . the Prime Minister. If it came out, you would be finished.'

e have to limit Jenkins' involvement in this affair without him knowing but also have to let Harris and the woman know that he has betrayed them?'

ave you ever met any of this unit before Prime Minister?'

'No, never.'

'Then don't start now sir, please. I'll check this Arab out and if you can contac
Blanch and ask him to see me at the hospital alone, I will arrange to meet Harri
and the Israeli.'

'What about *your* career detective, if all this came out?'

'Well then, natural deduction will point to the only other man who knew of an
such arrangements.'

'And who is that?'

'His wife does a great Hungarian Goulash?'

The PM smiled and held up his arms in mock despair. 'What about Blanch?'

'He's not going to tell anyone that he sponsored a government vigilante unit. N
more polo meetings with Bonny Prince Charlie, I would guess?'

'You are an unusual man!'

'Unusual Prime Minister, sir.'

'You have been a breath of fresh air, I am indebted to you.'

'My pleasure, sir.'

'Why have you been so . . . what's the word . . . forthcoming and of such unorthodox use?'

'Because it's my job and I love this country and its people and . . .'

'And?'

'I don't like bad guys so much, sir. I fucking hate them.'

The PM wandered over to the window to speak with his back to his new found ally. 'I am going to ask you a hypothetical question, Maurice?'

'Yes sir?'

'What do you really think of our denial unit?'

Peters knew where the question led. 'I would prefer it if we didn't have to use them but as long as they were our "dogs of war" and they saved British lives, then who am I to disagree with my elected leaders?'

'Would you have assisted them in their actions?'

'In this present crisis, yes sir.'

'And their previous actions against lawless factions?'

'I would prefer not to answer that sir.'

The PM turned from the window. 'Okay, I can respect that. I appreciate your honesty and I now find myself trusting you . . . though I only know you a few days.'

'Thank you, sir.'

'The Commissioner and, Jim Brannigan I must say, praised you as being someone who knew instinctively if someone was guilty or not. How so?'

'I'm flattered but not quite sure regarding their compliments.'

'Both men said you could walk onto a crime scene and get into the mind of the victim, and the killer.'

'I guess I have a good instinct, sir.'

'Do I love my wife, Detective Peters?'

The police officer was stunned but answered confidently. 'Without a doubt, you do love your wife.'

'Why so sure, a lot of couples, especially those in the spotlight, play out the charade for the media and the public.'

'I pick up on things sir. You are honest with her which leads me to believe that there is a significant bond between you.'

'Explain?'

earlier, you said that she would be thrilled to hear that someone did not recognise her *infamous* Goulash. You tell her the truth. Instead of *famous* you used *infamous* to describe her dish?'

Uncanny! You would make a fine politician Peters!' The PM said as he clapped him on the shoulder. 'Did you vote for me by the way?'

No sir, not a chance. I think your party surrendered its values to form a coalition and gain government. I am a bit of a socialist, I'm afraid.'

Hmm, there's a lot of truth around today. Let me call Blanch and tell him you're on the way to see him.'

And ask him to keep it to himself sir?'

Naturally Maurice.'

And sir?'

Yes?' The PM asked with the phone in his hand.

Remember this Prime Minister. If we establish that the injured Arab on the bridge, Khuram Abboud, is somehow connected to the terror plot, we have our sheikh.'

The PM replaced the phone without dialling. 'You'll have to explain that one to me?'

'Saudi succession is chaotic at present. If the bridge victim is involved, whoever sanctioned his diplomatic status in Riyadh-'

'You are fucking clever Peters. Wow!'

'Who could you trust sir, to uncover that information?'

'Well Jenkins, *the fuck*, is our mole so I think I can relax a bit and get MI6 to make enquiries. They have their uses you know Maurice.'

'Just before you call Blanch, sir?'

The PM replaced the phone in the cradle once more. 'Hit me?'

'We are assuming that whoever interfered with the camera monitoring your office was Jenkins?'

'It could have been a technical glitch, but go on?'

'Would anyone else have had the knowledge or capability to do that?'

The PM sat on the edge of the sofa next to the elegant phone table. 'You think there might be more than one mole in Cobra?'

'All I am saying is that I never accept the obvious. We might have a lead and say this in all humility, but the two of us have latched onto it-'

'You mean, you have.'

'Whatever sir, but seeing as you have got this far using a stranger to Cobra, meaning me, why not use someone new to garner the Saudi diplomatic link?'

'Like who?'

'That, I don't know Prime Minister but surely you have favours you can call in?'

'You mean the bloody CIA, don't you Maurice?'

Peters shrugged his shoulders.

'Maurice . . . I am speechless! However, we have come this far . . .'

'So why not use a non-Cobra, non-government approach.'

'What about the Israeli woman from the unit Maurice, any thoughts? She must have resources in that region?'

'And they call me Columbo?'

'I thought your nickname was Monk, television's other mysterious sleuth?'

'I've been called a lot of things sir.'

'And I haven't, you try doing this job?' The PM grinned and dialled the hospital direct. 'Half the population think I'm a complete prick!'

Peters dislodged a piece of meat from an awkward molar and took in the unreal situation once more. *This is weird!*

# CHAPTER TWENTY

Before DCI Peters left Downing Street via the garden exit, he placed a call to his Commissioner via Scotland Yard who rerouted a message back to Downing Street where the Cobra committee were gathering to begin their meeting. The purpose of the message was twofold - to misinform his immediate superior that he was being seen by a doctor with a case of suspected appendicitis and to suggest that he should bring in another detective while he was unable to attend the meetings.

After the Prime Minister entered the Cobra suite, the member's phones were once again placed in the basket and the Commissioner addressed the table.

'I'm afraid to say we are another man short, Prime Minister. Detective Chief Inspector Peters has a health issue. I believe he is going for a scan at the moment and I was thinking of getting another officer down here to help us-'

'That will not be necessary Commissioner, for the time being,' the PM butted in 'we can move ahead as we are but keep us informed of his health, if you would.'

The Home Secretary cleared his throat, attracting the required attention. 'May I presume to ask an awkward question?'

The PM nodded.

ask this in all innocence gentlemen, but has Peters' sudden illness got anything do with the witch-hunt phone issue we seem to have had?'

Vhat?' The MI6 head asked curiously.

Vell, to put it bluntly . . . was it Peters' phone that was bugged and leaked our iefings?'

bsolutely not!' The Commissioner raged. 'DCI Peters is a shrewd, loyal and reful officer.'

ie Deputy Prime Minister grabbed his moment. 'I heard that Peters paid a visit Cheltenham's GCHQ? What does that imply?'

ie PM snatched his moment. 'He actually drove down at my suggestion ntlemen.'

e did?' The Commissioner asked, caught unawares.

bsolutely,' the PM responded. 'Seeing as he was the stranger amongst us, I ought he had better take his mobile down there to have it checked by experts.'

ie same one he has used since we brought him into our confidence sir?' The 5 man asked tongue in cheek.

'Correct. I had my private secretary check the serial number to make sure.' The PM replied with relish, wondering how the deputy PM had heard about the visit to Cheltenham.

Bernard Jenkins eyed his boss with concern; something was not right. The PM suspected someone of being the mole and it was not DCI Maurice Peters. He would try to keep a low profile at this briefing. Years of civil service dealing with politicians and their intel lackeys had left him nauseous. The Sheikh was paying him a fortune to destabilise Cobra and the country in general and while he regretted the carnage of recent days, he hoped the situation would alert the politicians to the dangers of the big bad world. Britain had become a poor relation; its superpower status thrown to the wolves. Putin and the jihadists were the only people taking action, besides the Sheikh who he actually admired. The West was weaker than it had ever been, much to do with the weakling in the White House who Bernard despised. He had given his life to his country, sitting back while inept governments came and went. He had earned a civil servant' pay for too long and it was just not worth it. Old age would hopefully see him retire somewhere expensive and safe to reflect on the fact that he too had been a man who took action. His thoughts came back to the briefing when he heard a familiar name spoken by the egotistical clown occupying the chair of MI, another bloody lackey.

huram Abboud is not the name of the man shot on Waterloo Bridge earlier
day,' the spook announced.

Vhat is his name?' The PM asked curiously.

Iakim Nassar, a Saudi national. He is the brother of the other Nassar who blew
mself into a crater in Feltham. We have a source inside the Saudi Embassy.'

nd he is a reliable source, gentlemen,' his MI6 counterpart added.

nd what do we infer from this?' The PM enquired, pouring himself a filtered
ffee.

e are not sure sir, but come on . . . it's hardly a coincidence?'

nkins was forced to input. 'Absolutely, well done gents. Now, we have to find
t what the link is between a Saudi national crossing Waterloo Bridge and the
ooting of Sir Raymond Blanch could be?'

e Prime Minister met Jenkins' enquiring gaze and forced a smile. *You fucking
t! Just you wait.*

ouldn't it have been random . . . the sniper trying to take away the focus of his
ack on Lord Blanch?' The Home Secretary asked.

'Well, there is that possibility sir,' Bernard Jenkins replied with a hint of scepticism. 'Snipers have been known to do that but, they have always been multiple targets. Let's keep our minds open here?'

The Deputy PM made his play. 'I keep thinking of what the CIA refer to as the anonymous assassin. But if he is active in all of this . . . what's his agenda?'

The debriefing turned in a new direction and after a longer than normal period without anything conclusive or constructive being agreed on, the PM muddied the waters, waiting for Jenkins to react.

'So some of you think that an Arab Sheikh, possibly Saudi Arabian, hired a hit man for something and the terror cells have been a diversion. Someone who also took down four of our disavowed unit?'

Jenkins bit. 'I wouldn't go that far Prime Minister-'

'Why not Bernard?' He replied lethargically.

'Well, it's just not cricket sir . . . a bloodthirsty jihadist hiring an infidel?'

'I tend to agree with Bernard sir,' the MI6 controller said. 'We are not yet certain that this assassin, if he is active, is a *Westerner* and if he is . . . I seriously doubt if he would have been hired by the jihadists who have slaughtered so many of our compatriots. These Arab lunatics have a code, a misguided code, but a code nevertheless.'

he Home Secretary joined in. 'But Detective Peters seemed sure that the
ssassin was an infidel, meaning a non-radical Muslim-'

et's leave Peters to concentrate on his appendicitis, shall we?' Jenkins
marked.

*otcha fucker!* The PM thought as he spilled his coffee onto his trousers.

ppendicitis?' The Deputy PM enquired, 'if that's what he has, we won't be
eing him back here for a while?'

ne Commissioner of the London Metropolitan Police Service did not react to
e previously unmentioned illness as he presumed that Jenkins had ears at
otland Yard. Ears everywhere.

hit,' the PM said, standing up to reveal the coffee stain spreading down his
ouser leg. 'Carry on with this. I'll be back after I change.'

\*

here are you right now Maurice?' The PM asked a few moments later using
s bedroom phone.

**ve just showed my alias ID to the uniforms here in St Thomas and I'm**
**out to go in and talk to Sir Raymond. What's up sir?'**

'Jenkins just gave himself away at Cobra with an *appendicitis* remark. Is he on to you?'

**'No chance sir, but I'd say he has a friend at Scotland Yard by the sound of it.'**

'You called the commissioner through the Yard's switchboard as we planned?'

**'Yes sir and they rerouted my messages to the commissioner before he went into Cobra.'**

'So you're not unduly worried by this?'

**'No sir. What was it like sitting in the same room as Jenkins?'**

'To be honest Maurice, I felt like reaching over and punching his rat face every time I looked at it.'

**'Bad idea sir, that just *might* give our game away.'**

'I know, it's just frustration speaking.'

**'Blanch's escort is approaching me as we speak, sir. Did Jenkins mention the unit or Harris?'**

'He is playing it cool Maurice. I am going to put a tail on him.'

**'Can I suggest someone really quickly?'**

Go on!'

**That guy Andrew, who I met at GCHQ? I know he is a tech chap but he is smart boss, very smart.'**

Another outsider.' The PM enthused before adding. 'You just called me boss?'

**Oh, sorry sir.'**

ah, I like it. Stay safe and I'll contact GCHQ before I go back in.'

Peters replayed the conversation over in his head as he was escorted into a private meeting with Sir Raymond Blanch. *Boss?* He was using a hastily prepared Special Branch pass under an alias to meet the tycoon, as arranged by the man who he had just called boss.

## CHAPTER TWENTY ONE

'Move, move . . . please!' A young doctor shouted at Peters and his two escort as they walked past an operating theatre. The medic took no notice of their ID badges as she was more concerned with her patient on the gurney that she was directing to theatre. A homeless man had been knocked down outside the hospital and had suffered a head trauma.

"We care for everyone here, not just your lords and ladies!" Peters heard her smart as he left behind the scene to enter a private room where Sir Raymond Blanch lay conscious on a bed that was leagues above the average hospital issue. There were already plenty of gifted flowers in the make-do room though no television as of yet. Blanch's two escorts, a stocky, fit looking man in his late thirties and a tanned, younger woman gave him the once-over.

'Thank you for seeing me Sir Raymond, at such short notice,' Peters said.

'Whatever the Prime Minister requests, Detective,' Blanch replied activating his head rest to gain a better view of his guest.

'And would the same go for you Mister Harris or do I address you as Captain Harris? I'm not sure what to call your former Mossad colleague either?'

Blanch's face reddened. 'You are not who that ID badge says you are, are you?

'No sir, the Prime Minister thought it better if I came here anonymously.'

215

're you carrying a weapon, Detective?' Sara Brahms asked just as Kenneth
arris walked over to frisk him.

m DCI Peters, madam. Please do whatever you have to do Captain?' Peters
id as he held up his arms.

hy the bloody subterfuge Peters. What are you and the PM up to?'

hat, Sir Raymond, has to remain confidential between him, you and I.'

e's not carrying a weapon Raymond,' Harris said to Blanch, awaiting his
cision.

ank you, Kenneth. Could you and Sara remain close by while I have a
ivate chat with this chap?'

o problem, we'll be outside.'

eep your distance from Special Branch and whoever else is out there. What
y don't know does not concern them.'

cup of tea boss?' Sara motioned to Harris as they departed the second storey
r recovery room.

ease take a seat, Detective?'

ank you, Sir Raymond. How are you holding up?'

bloody painful but it could have been worse, don't you think?'

'No sir, I do not. If the sniper wanted to kill you, we wouldn't be talking.'

'Of course Peters, just testing you. So, what's the verdict?'

'May I ask what you and Harris and the woman . . .?'

'Sara Brahms is her name, a great intelligence asset to have.'

'But not that great considering what happened today sir, in all due respect to th
lady and her capabilities.'

'That's why they are here now, to discuss this mess. There was absolutely n
way to foresee this happening.'

'Who do you think shot you and killed your other four unit members S
Raymond?'

'Firstly, stop with the "Sir" stuff. I'm in a hospital bed and you are here to hel
so please address me as Raymond . . . or Blanch, or whatever! Just give n
what you and the PM have got? Was the man who was shot on Waterloo Brid
an Albanian?'

'No sir, he was not.'

'Same bullet type as that what got me though!'

'Oh?'

'Well, out with it man?'

You are not going to like my reply sir but I have to be blunt.'

Blunt is good Peters, I do blunt also. Contrary to media opinion, I am not the publicity seeking, ruthless big shot that they would have people think I am. I can't abide "yes" men, so please, be brutally blunt.'

Okay Raymond. *I* am here to ask *you* questions, not the reverse, not yet anyhow. The questions might even seem pointless but just trust me that they are relevant.'

said blunt, not callous, man.'

As I said, you wouldn't like my reply. Can I continue now?'

Yes, of course. Would you like a cup of tea or something while we chat Detective?'

I would actually, if it's okay with you.'

Kenneth!' Blanch managed to shout, 'Sara?'

A short uneasy silence followed.

They might be at the nurse's station Peters, can you pop your head out and check?'

Of course.'

Peters pulled the door handle and peered in each direction. 'They are not her Raymond.' He withdrew back into the room. 'There are four armed Specia Branch officers outside so do you want-'

'I would like a cuppa Detective, same as you. Would you chase off and scrambl up two cups and tell Kenneth and Sara that we will be chatting a while?'

'Yes, Raymond. It feels all kinds of wrong calling a Lord by his first name b the way.'

'Like it or lump it man! Oh, reminds me, two lumps of sugar, no milk.'

\*\*\*

'Don't *fucking* move a muscle. I'll squeeze this trigger without blinking.' Sa Brahms said as she held her Browning semi-automatic on the homeless ma who had been brought into St Thomas' Hospital.

Kenneth Harris crept up the stairwell from the floor beneath as the duo boxe the man in. The vagrant had awoken in the examination room and aft demanding to leave, he had become aggressive towards the medical team. appeared his head wound was a scam to grab a bed for the night. The examini doctor had found red dye instead of blood on his scalp. He had also concealed bottle of mentholated spirits within his grubby overcoat and was still the wor for wear from it. After quickly checking the CCTV footage of the hospi

recourt, the medical staff ascertained that he had merely nudged himself
ainst a passing motorist. The armed officers ignored the fracas to concentrate
Blanch and their Arab patient.

the homeless man was being led away by a porter, he slumped against
nneth Harris at the coffee machine and whispered coherently into his ear.

ast stairwell, Harris?"

rris and Sara watched as the man ran off, pursued by a hospital porter. The
ne porter now lay unconscious on the stairwell beside the exit door. The
neless man had removed his cumbersome coat and stood alert as Sara kept
weapon on him.

ep your gun on him Sara!' Harris shouted as he climbed steadily towards the
e-off.

ll do boss!' Sara shouted, tightening her grip on the Browning. 'I'll drop him
hout a thought.'

ris arrived behind the foul smelling man with his own Sauer 226 semi
nted at the man who knew his name and who was not in the least bit
xicated.

o are you?' Kenneth asked as he proceeded to inspect the man for weapons.

'Not who, why.' The assassin replied casually. His hair was grey and matted and his skin appeared jaundiced. Make-up.

'What do you mean, why?'

'Why I came here, hoping to meet you Captain Harris . . . and Miss Brahm there.'

'Which is?'

'To tell you that I am no longer targeting you both and to warn you-'

'What the fuck!' Harris was alarmed. 'Are you the shooter . . . did you kill o friends?'

'Unfortunately and regrettably, yes.'

Former SAS Captain Kenneth Harris lunged forward to strike the man acro the head with his weapon.

He got within inches before the assassin grabbed his wrist in an Aiki adducted wristlock and spun him violently into Sara who crashed against wall. As Harris went for his fallen weapon, he received a heel into his sternu The movement was over before it began. The surprise factor always came i play, rarely giving anyone time to blink.

ara looked up at the stranger. 'Who are you?' She made no attempt to reach for er own automatic on the floor.

/ith Harris immobilised, the killer bent down and looked her in the eye. 'I ean you two no harm. There is an injured Arab here in this hospital who orks for a Sheikh who hired-'

'ou bastard!' Harris groaned as he tried to catch his breath. From beneath his aistline, he pulled out a hidden revolver and was steadying himself to aim.

on't do it!' The killer warned, his eyes dull, ready to react.

uck you!' Were the last words Kenneth Harris spoke as he pressed on the gger.

uck you Bubba!'

e assassin, though crouched, spun around with a reverse kick that caught arris full on the chin. The Ushiro Geri Shotokan back kick carried deadly rce when properly applied. Harris' head rebounded off the wall to the echo of e shot that had embedded itself into the exit door. He was dead before he mped to the cement landing. Sara looked at the killer as he twisted himself ck to confront her. For the first time in years, the ex Mossad agent thought her ne was up. The man's dull eyes betrayed his profession - death.

'You had your chance, Mossad. I tried to mend things with you and Harris despite what I've done so far. Goodbye and good luck. You are going to need it.

Then he was gone, through the bullet marked exit and she was alone, a deathl awareness pervading her thoughts.

The End

Anthony Vincent Bruno

© 2014

# BOOKS BY ANTHONY VINCENT BRUNO

THE WICKED WILL PERISH 1 – SAS: BODY COUNT

THE WICKED WILL PERISH 2 – HELL HATH NO FURY

THE WICKED WILL PERISH 3 – THE ASSASSIN

THE WICKED WILL PERISH 4 – NO PRISONERS

THE WICKED WILL PERISH 5 – SAS BELLATOR

----------

And then some ONE

And then some TWO

----------

COURAGE

HOLDING ON

THE PSYCHIC KILLER

SEX, LIES AND THE BOMB

NEVER AGAIN

Printed in Great Britain
by Amazon

49510740R00137